When
the Sirens
Wailed

Other books by Noel Streatfeild

THURSDAY'S CHILD
BALLET SHOES
THE CHILDREN ON THE TOP FLOOR
CIRCUS SHOES
DANCING SHOES
THE FAMILY AT CALDICOTT PLACE
FAMILY SHOES
THE MAGIC SUMMER
MOVIE SHOES
NEW SHOES
QUEEN VICTORIA
SKATING SHOES
THEATER SHOES
TRAVELING SHOES

Noel Streatfeild

When the Sirens Wailed

Illustrated by Judith Gwyn Brown

Random House New York

First American Edition

Copyright © 1976 by Noel Streatfeild. Illustrations Copyright © 1976 by Random House, Inc. All rights reserved under International and Pan-American Copyright Conventions. Published in the United States by Random House, Inc., New York. Originally published in Great Britain as WHEN THE SIREN WAILED by William Collins Sons & Co., Ltd., London. Copyright © 1974 by Noel Streatfeild.

Library of Congress Cataloging in Publication Data

Streatfeild, Noel. When the sirens wailed. SUMMARY: Rather than stay with a new family, three young evacuees try to return to their home in London after their country host dies suddenly.
  [1. World War, 1939–1945—Great Britain—Fiction]   I. Title.   PZ7.S914Wh5   [Fic]
75–38326   ISBN 0–394–83147–0   ISBN 0–394–93147–5 lib. bdg.

Manufactured in the United States of America   1 2 3 4 5 6 7 8 9 0

For Iolanthe Owen
with love

Editor's Note

The British monetary system is different from the American. The British use pounds instead of dollars. In September 1939 (the time of this story) a pound equaled about $4.00 in American money, and there were 20 shillings in a pound. This meant that a shilling was worth about 20¢. A crown was equal to 5 shillings—about $1.00—so a half-crown was approximately the same as 50¢ in American money.

At the time of World War II there were 12 pennies in a shilling. Thus a sixpenny piece—half a shilling—was worth about 10¢, and 3 pennies were equal to 5¢. At first this was all very confusing to American soldiers, but they soon learned to use the new kind of currency, and the British merchants were extremely helpful—and patient—in explaining its value.

Contents

When
the Sirens
Wailed

The Departure

THE CLARK family lived in a house in South London. They thought it was a nice house, for in the 1930s, when this story happened, people were pleased with a lot less than they are today. There was a front parlor, a kitchen, and two bedrooms. What was known as "the Privy" was outside and shared with other families. There was no bath but a big tub in which they all had baths on Saturday nights. There was no water piped into the house but in the kitchen there was a pump that brought in water from the water-butt, which stood outside the kitchen door. It was all wrong that they had no tap water, but their house, like all the others in the street, had been condemned for years, so it might have fallen to pieces for any trouble the landlord took with it. Fortunately the children's father, whose name was Edward though he was always called Nobby, was very handy with tools and patched the house up as best he could with no money when anything went wrong.

Money—or rather the lack of it—was something that was always there. Nobody spoke about it more than they could help, but it was like a dying mouse in a cupboard. You knew it was there but somehow it hurt less if you did not open the cupboard door to look. Many people were pitiably poor in the 1930s. "No point in grousing about it" was Nobby's philosophy. Most Thursdays, for Thursday was the poorest day of the week—part-time pay was fetched on Fridays—Rosie, the children's mother, would say, "Potato dinner again today. There's one big potato each for you kids and the water they're boiled in for your dad and me. Try to stop the boys saying anything about being hungry, Laura. It upsets your dad."

There were three Clark children: Laura, who was nine when this story starts; Andy, who was seven, and Tim, who was five. Laura was a pretty blue-eyed child so sometimes, especially on Saturdays, Rosie would send her to the shops because occasionally she could get little extras Rosie could not. Oh, the pride Laura felt when she could run home with a bone with real meat on it or, as had happened once, a gift of a sausage.

Nobby, who was a docker, was by nature a cheerful little cock sparrow of a man, so it took a lot to get him down.

"There's many worse off than us," he would point out when times were extra hard. "They say up in the north the workers are downright starving! And one thin' we do 'ave what is worth more'n money any day, we got a 'appy 'ome." This was true, for in the Clarks' tumble-down house there was a lot of love.

Being poor, and even being hungry, was something you could get used to; but being afraid and having no one to talk to about it was something new and Laura could not get used to it. She had tried to talk to her mother the awful day when they were fitted with their gas masks, but she never explained properly. All her life Laura had been scared of being shut up, and that was just what a gas mask did to her. It was clamped over your face and there you were with your head in a sort of prison.

It was a Saturday morning when Rosie took them all to the Town Hall.

"Now we don't want no complainin'," she said. "These masks what we're to have are free, a present like."

"Why do we want 'em, Mum?" Andy asked.

Rosie seemed to think about that.

"It's the Germans," she said. "If there was a war—which your dad says there won't be—there could be stuff dropped which is bad to sniff up. Well, these masks what we're to have, we'd wear then."

Laura shivered.

"Who'd tell us to put them on and when to take them off?"

Rosie had no idea, but she was not going to admit it. She had heard her mother speak of men on bicycles warning the public of zeppelin raids in the First World War. Doubtless the same system would work for gas.

"Men on bicycles," she said with false conviction, "ride up our street they will and call out to put the things on."

"And then come back and tell us to take them off?" Laura asked.

"Course," said Rosie with even more false conviction.

In the Town Hall, with dozens of other flustered mums and their families, the Clarks followed the arrows which said GAS MASKS. When they reached the gas-mask room they found at one end long trestle tables behind which were sitting rows of men wearing blue coveralls and hats made of tin with a W painted on the front. Behind them were great piles of cardboard boxes.

All the waiting families were formed into lines so as they moved forward they could see what was going on. Out of the boxes came things which were rather like ugly dress-up masks. They were made of black india rubber with a round metal nose that stuck out. For little children like Tim, who was only four at the time, there was another sort of mask that looked like a Mickey Mouse face. Laura thought the Mickey Mouse kind was worse than the black kind, for Mickey Mouse was meant to be a friendly character. Now, turned into a mask and clamped over the small children's faces, he became horrible. When the little children were forced to try on the masks for size they let out screams that could be heard a block away.

When the Clark family reached the trestle table Rosie bent down to whisper to the children. "If there's a peep out of one of you your dad will take his belt to you when he comes home." Dad never had taken his belt to any of them and the children knew it, but they would not have made a fuss even if Rosie had not added, "And there'll be a sweet each for those who 'ave be'aved nice when we get outside."

After the gas-mask fittings were over, the gas-mask cases were slung on their tapes over the children's shoulders. Most of the children felt they were rather smart.

"Now," said the man in coveralls who had fitted them, "from this minute, whatever you are doing, you don't leave the house without that box. Sometime, you won't never know when, I shall call at your school and say 'Gas masks on,' and what do you think will happen to the boy or girl what has left theirs at 'ome or, worse still, lost it?"

"You'll take a strap to them," Andy suggested.

Rosie was bitterly ashamed.

"Don't talk so silly, Andy. No one hasn't never taken a strap to you."

The man gave Rosie an understanding smile.

"No strap," he told Andy, "but the sharp edge of me tongue, and I wouldn't wonder if the school didn't make you write out fifty times 'I must always carry my gas mask.' "

Where Rosie found the halfpenny for three sweets only she knew, but the candy did its work. Outside, chewing their sweets, marching down the road with gas-mask boxes swinging, the fittings seemed like a bad dream. Even Laura cheered up. The gas masks were out of view. Perhaps they weren't really in the boxes at all; there was no need to open them to see. Particularly she didn't want Mum's box opened, for when the man in coveralls had put Mum's head in a mask it had been worse than anything. Instead of being Mum, she had changed into the sort of creature that advertised horror films on the posters.

"What would that man really do if I lost my gas mask?" Andy asked.

Rosie laughed.

"Put you in the Tower of London, shouldn't wonder!"

After a time gas masks became so much a part of all children that, except for occasional examinations by the men who had fitted them, they were forgotten.

Even Laura stopped thinking about the horrible things. Dad was always saying they were a waste of the country's money, for they would never be needed, and Dad was nearly always right. It was other things that made Laura feel as though she had lumps of ice in her tummy. Secret things that were going on. They began with letters from the school to bring home to Mum and Dad. The letters were taken by Mum and put on the shelf in the kitchen for Dad when he came in.

Whatever was in the letters was never discussed before the children. But what *could* be in them? Laura knew it couldn't be a complaint about her work, for she was doing well; she often got a star on her compositions. And it wasn't Andy; he was the opposite of her, never shy of anybody and always said what he thought. But he didn't do anything bad like hurting smaller boys, certainly nothing that would mean sending home a letter. Twice Laura was driven by fright to creep down after she was supposed to be in bed to listen in to what her parents were saying. It was easy to hear for the door didn't fit. The first time it was about suitcases.

"There's no way by which I could raise money for suitcases," Laura heard her father say. "There's nothing left to pawn and what sticks of furniture we got wouldn't fetch nothin' even if we could manage without 'em."

Rosie seemed to be looking at the letter delivered to her that day by Laura.

"It says those what haven't got suitcases can use pillowcases. But I 'aven't got those neither nor nothing I could cut up to make them. As you know, all them went months ago. All we got is blankets and not enough of them."

Nobby knew about the blankets. Gently, for Rosie was proud and hated to parade her poverty, he said, "They do say carrier bags will do. And it may not be far. Why, it could be Brighton."

Laura had to scuttle back to bed then for her father moved as if he might be going to open the door, but she lay awake a long time worrying. Why would they want paper carrier bags? They were for shopping in stores. And where was Brighton?

The second time was worse, for Laura heard her mother

crying, not just quiet tears but great sobs dragged out of her.

"I'm sorry, Nobby," she gasped between the sobs, "but I can't bear to let them go and that's a fact."

Laura shivered. Where were they going and why?

Dad seemed to be holding Mum, for his voice was muffled as if he were speaking into her neck.

"Give over, luv! I keep telling you there's no need for you to stay. I'll manage. You know it said on that first paper, 'Mothers with children of school age or under can be evacuated.' "

That checked Rosie's sobs.

"Nobby Clark," she gasped, "if you think I'm leavin' you alone 'ere while I go off you've another think comin'."

Dad said, "You know what I told you. If it 'appens—and it still never may—it's the navy for me."

"I know," Rosie agreed. "And I told you, even if you went into the navy, I was staying here. Our 'ome may not be much but it's all we got and someone's got to look after it, so when it's over we can all be together again."

Then suddenly there were no secrets any more. Everybody knew what was going to happen. There was going to be a war and while it lasted, which probably wouldn't be long, all children in danger areas like London were to be sent to the country. Then rehearsals started. The children had to come to school each with a suitcase, pillowcase, or carrier bag. In it there was to be only what each child could carry, which in Tim's case was very little indeed. They all, of course, had their gas-mask boxes slung across their shoulders. On each child was pinned with a big safety pin a piece of paper with his name, address, and the name of his school on it. Each child also had a stamped postcard addressed to his or her parents to be sent off with the new address immediately on arrival. These rehearsals happened several times and became a kind of game, for none of the children could imagine being sent away from their dads and mums.

Then on Friday, September 1, 1939, it happened. There was what the children supposed was yet another rehearsal, only this one was called much earlier in the morning than usual. As soon as they arrived at the school, it was clear that this time the practice was for real. For one thing Dad and Mum came with them to the school. Then out of Dad's pocket came presents: for Laura a tiny doll, for Andy a ball, and for Tim a small duck to float in a bath. Small cheap toys, but all that Dad and Mum could afford. Almost no time was wasted that day. The children were formed into a straggling procession, and even while they were giving their parents a last kiss they were marching off to the station. Few children cried, for what was happening didn't seem real. Laura didn't cry because she had Tim to drag along. He wanted to stay there and play with his duck. But if the children didn't cry, some of the mothers did as they followed the procession all the way to the railway station.

At the station the children were divided into groups and put into trains. Going where?

Rosie, choking back her tears, managed to be heard by Laura as she called through the window, "Good-by, kids. Don't forget to post your address. And see you look after the boys, Laura. They're in your charge now."

Charnbury

I T W A S a long journey; at least it seemed long to the hot, sticky, often trainsick children. The evacuation, named Operation Pied Piper, had been planned for at least a year and worked on ever since. On that Friday—and during the next two days—827,000 schoolchildren were evacuated to so-called safe areas all over the country. So, of course, where any family was sent was just a matter of luck. The three Clark children might have been part of the group that went all the way to their destination by bus, or even three of the 23,000 who went by pleasure steamers to places on the East Coast, but instead their group was sent to the West Country.

On the train there were two grownups in charge of the Clark children's group of forty-six children. They gave each child a sandwich and a cup of milk; they provided a basin and comforted the trainsick. Each coachload of children was completely cut off from those in the rest of the train. All through the journey the train stopped at different stations, and long queues, or lines, of children, clutching their luggage, were marched off somewhere by their grownups. Laura, her nose glued to the window, had hard work not to cry. Soon they would be part of a queue. But going where?

Laura, Andy, and Timothy were not trainsick. Laura had felt peculiar and had been unable to eat her sandwich, but Andy had wolfed it so the ladies hadn't noticed. She had been kept too busy by Tim to have time to be trainsick. The train had only just left London when Tim said, "Laura, Tim wants to go 'ome."

Laura had put an arm round him.

"You can't go 'ome yet, Tim," she explained. "We're goin' on a 'oliday first."

But though Laura tried in every way to amuse him Tim would not be comforted. Instead, louder and louder he kept up his sad cries. "I want to go 'ome. I wants our mum."

Fortunately, after about an hour of this, Tim grew tired and, lolling against Laura, he fell asleep.

Andy on the whole enjoyed the journey. He and several other small boys invented a game in which one side of the carriage was fighting the other. This caused the boys to make sudden dives across the carriage with the object of dragging an enemy boy to the ground, which usually meant that the boys were fighting on the floor while the girls shouted, "Don't be so rough!" or "You kicked me!" or sometimes called to the grownups for help.

Then one of the ladies in charge would separate the offending boys and put them back on their seats, but peace didn't last long. Two more were soon fighting.

Suddenly there was a change. The ladies clapped their hands and called for silence. Then one of them produced a sheet of paper covered with names.

"We are now in the county of Dorset," she explained, "the county in which all of you are going to live. Our next stop will be a place called Charnbury. I will now read out the names of all you children who are to get out there. So please each child, as I call out your name, answer 'Here.' Then hang your gas-mask cases over your shoulders and collect your luggage ready to follow me when the train stops."

The lady read out a long list of names and each child answered "Here." Soon she came to Andrew Clark and Timothy Clark, followed by John Donald. There was no mention of Laura Clark.

Laura felt as if her inside was turning over. They couldn't be separated. Mum had said she was to look after the boys. But what should she do? The ladies were all-powerful. If they said she was to go to a different place, could they make her?

Surprisingly it was Andy who spoke up.

"Me an' Tim aren't goin' nowhere, not without Laura comes along of us."

The ladies hurried down the coach.

"Who is Laura?" the one who had read the list asked.

Andy sounded scornful.

"She's our sister a'course."

The other lady, who had noticed with gratitude the way Laura had handled Tim, said, "So your name is Clark?"

"That's right," Laura agreed. "There's three of us, see."

The ladies went into a huddle. Then the one with the list said, "I don't know how this mistake occurred but we must try and arrange that you aren't separated from your brothers. I shall add your name to this list. I am sure whoever is offering a home to the boys will be glad to have you too. Now get your things and hold the little boy's hand. I will lift him out of the train."

Charnbury was a largish village. It was, like most of Dorset, a very pretty place. There were trees everywhere and flowers in all the gardens, even some flowers growing in the station itself. As the children trailed along behind the lady with the list, they pointed out to each other lovely flowers growing in the cottage gardens. A man came past them driving a piebald pony pulling a cart full of sacks. He gave them a wave with his whip.

"Hullo, kids!" he called out. "Welcome to Charnbury!"

Even the most frightened cheered up a little.

The foster parents were waiting for the children in a hall known as the Scouts' Hut. A brisk woman to whom most of the children took an instant dislike greeted them.

"I am Miss Justworthy, your billeting officer. If you children will sit on the floor I will introduce you to your hosts. Now don't forget my name. Say it all together: 'Good afternoon, Miss Justworthy.' "

All the children, even the smallest, did what they were told. They were too scared to do anything else.

It was unlucky that the children were not the only ones who did not care for Miss Justworthy. The foster parents did not like her either. They were willing, or at least had accepted it as their duty, to take in the children, but they would have liked to choose their own visitors and to say how many, and of what sex, they would have. Instead Miss Justworthy had insisted on coming into their homes and, having seen the accommodation, had told the householder how many of what sex she was to accept.

"*I* wouldn't mind a little old boy," one woman had said. "But my mother who lives with us is not so young any more. So couldn't I have a quiet little girl?"

Miss Justworthy just hadn't listened, but had written on

her list in a final way, "two boys."

The foster parents were sitting at the far end of the room. Each was trying to wear what he or she—it was mostly shes —hoped was a welcoming face. But they were local people, many of them the wives of farm laborers. Although they read newspapers when they had time, they had not—until they saw the children—known what years of unemployment did to people.

Most mothers, including Rosie, had done their best to send their children away looking decent. The boys' shorts had as a rule started the day clean, and jerseys, though pitiably thin, were carefully darned. Few carried overcoats because they had been pawned. Nobby was hoping to get his children's out before the winter. Laura had a navy blue frock which Rosie had bought in a rummage sale specially for the evacuation. At home the frock had looked good, even smart, but to the Dorset housewives it was a poor little washed-out rag of a dress.

The worst, though, was how the children looked.

There had been nowhere to wash on the train. Every child needed a good scrub, and it was of baths that most of the women were thinking.

The train lady who had the list was talking to Miss Justworthy.

"It can't be managed," Miss Justworthy snapped. "I was told to expect forty-five children of eleven or under and forty-five children of eleven or under I have billeted. And it's not been easy. You can have no idea!"

The other train lady, the one who hadn't the list, said, "Don't let's separate the family."

Miss Justworthy evidently cared nothing for families.

"I can't help it. He asked for two boys and two boys he's

going to have—Andrew and Timothy."

At that moment the door of the hall was flung open and in stalked an old man. He was the most impressive old man many of the children had ever seen. In spite of being old he had a completely straight back and he was over six feet tall. His iron-gray hair was immaculately tidy and his face was the color of a purple plum. He was dressed in a tweed suit which looked as if it was part of him.

"Afternoon, all," he said.

There was a subdued murmur of, "Afternoon, Squire," from the foster parents.

The old man looked at the tired, dirty children sitting on the floor and whatever he had meant to say he swallowed. Instead he asked Miss Justworthy in a severe voice, "What's holding things up? What these children want is a good meal and a bath in that order."

The foster parents moved as if ready to take the child or children allotted to them and go. They were stopped by Miss Justworthy.

"There is a hitch, Squire. I was told to find billets for forty-*five* schoolchildren of eleven and under and I have done so. We have been sent forty-*six* children."

The Squire clearly thought nothing of Miss Justworthy.

"Madam," he said, "you are the billeting officer and must make the necessary arrangements. Give me my two boys and we will go."

Miss Justworthy was clearly glad she had a smart answer for him.

"It is your two boys who are the trouble. They have a sister and they say they won't be separated from her."

The Squire did not show a sign of what he might be thinking.

"Tell the boys to stand up."

Miss Justworthy shouted in a military way, "Andrew and Timothy Clark, stand up."

Andy was on his feet at once, but Tim had gone to sleep again and Laura had to wake him. The Squire could see Tim was not conscious of what was going on, so he gave all his attention to Andy.

"Is your name Andrew Clark?"

Andy ranked the old man with schoolmasters, so he spoke respectfully.

"Yes, sir, but I'm called Andy."

The Squire pointed to Laura, who still held Tim's hand.

"Is that your sister?"

"Yes, sir. That's Laura. And Tim and me aren't going nowhere without her.

The Squire fixed his faded blue eyes on Laura.

"Why did you not get listed for evacuation with your brothers?"

Laura was worried about Tim. He looked a funny color and might at any moment do something he shouldn't, one end or the other.

"I was on the list," she said. "It's just she's"—she pointed to the lady with the list—"got me left out. Please, sir, could I take Tim outside? I think he wants to go somewhere."

Everyone was relieved when Laura and Tim were out of sight. The Squire, however, was turning things over in his mind. He had been a regular soldier and in those days had acquired a soldier servant known as a batman. When he left the army he took his soldier servant with him as butler-gardener-chauffeur-odd-job man. Pretty soon the man, whose name was Elk, had married and his wife also had become part of the household. She was the same age as Elk, and Elk was the same age as his master, so they were an elderly household.

When the news of the evacuation reached the Squire he had sent for Mr. and Mrs. Elk.

"It's about this evacuation. Have to do our bit, of course. How many could we take?"

The house was small for what was then called a gentleman's residence. There was the front room, in which the Squire slept, a little dressing room off it, a spare room with two beds, and three living rooms. A bedroom and bathroom had been built on beyond the kitchen for the Elks.

"There's the two beds in the spare room, sir," Elk had said.

Then Mrs. Elk had spoken up. "They'll have to be boys, sir. This is a bachelor establishment. There's no place for girls."

So when Miss Justworthy and her lists had arrived she had received her orders from the Squire.

"I will take two boys. This is a bachelor establishment."

But the Squire, however he might look, did not have a heart of iron; he thought the evacuees pathetic. So now he said to Andy, "I'll take the three of you just for tonight." He turned to fix stern eyes on Miss Justworthy. "This arrangement is for one night only. You will call to see me tomorrow at ten o'clock sharp. I am not giving a home to the girl."

Small Hall

THOMAS ELK had made no mistake when he had asked
Martha Godstone to marry him. She had run the house
her father lived in efficiently and well since her mother's
death eight years earlier. Her father, before he retired, had
been a lawyer's clerk, a responsible, respectable calling, and
he expected his home to match it. Martha's mother had
provided this until her death and Martha had carried on
from there. Everything kept spotless and unchanging and
good meals served exactly to time.

The Squire's family had lived in Charnbury for five
hundred years. They had not greatly distinguished themselves, but they had been good landlords, and their wives and
sisters had been tireless in looking after those who needed
help. Each year for many years they had grown poorer, and
each generation had been forced to sell land, so that by the
time the First World War started they were only holding
onto the family home by their eyelashes. The war had
finished the family as landlords. All the young men of the
family were killed and the heir, who was a regular soldier
called Colonel Launcelot Stranger Stranger, came home to

find The Hall falling to pieces. He had, however, been able to sell the land on which it had stood. With the money, he had bought a cottage, added onto it, made a garden, and christened the place "Small Hall." And when he had leave from the army he and his batman Elk had camped out there.

At about the same time they both retired from the army, Elk discovered Martha and asked her to marry him. The three had lived there happily ever since. It makes for happiness when everybody wants the same things: perfect tidiness, a place for everything and everything in its place, good plain English cooking, and all strictly on schedule.

To the village it made no difference at all if Colonel Stranger Stranger lived in The Hall or a converted cottage. He was still called the Squire just as his ancestors had been before him. That morning when he had driven off to the Scouts' Hut, driving his old but beautifully kept station wagon, Martha had said to Elk, "We're going to see changes here, Thomas Elk. We shall have to pray we accept them with resignation and make the boys happy."

Elk was not downhearted.

"You never served the Colonel except in this house. But me I've served him half over the world. No matter how bad things were he always got order in two or three days. It will be the same with these two boys. He'll soon get them into his ways, you see if he don't."

The three Clarks had not supposed they could feel more bewildered than they did but that was before they saw the station wagon. They had never driven in a car!

"Aren't that smashin'!" Andy exclaimed.

The Colonel, though determined only to put up with Laura for one night, was as a rule polite to women.

"You sit beside me," he said to her. "You two boys hop

into the back." Tim at once began to howl, "I wants to sit with Laura."

Laura looked anxiously at the Colonel.

" 'E's just throw'd up," she said. " 'E'll be better along of me."

The Colonel believed in starting as you intended to go on.

"Nonsense! Timothy, get in and stop that noise."

He did not say it unkindly but was just giving an order he expected to have obeyed.

Timothy, feeling ill and scared, knew nothing of orders and continued to wail unceasingly all the way to Small Hall.

"I wan'a go 'ome. I want me mum. I want Laura."

Timothy might not have been making a sound for all the interest the Colonel took.

"I expect you little people are hungry," he said politely to Laura, "and you can certainly do with a bath."

Elk and Martha met the car at the front door. So that there was no mistake the Colonel at once handed Laura to Martha.

"There has been some muddle which Miss Justworthy is straightening out. This is the boys' sister, Laura, who will be with us for one night only."

Martha had tea ready for them in the kitchen. A simple meal of bacon and eggs, but to the Clark children born in an age of unemployment it was a feast. Three kinds of cake, watercress, a great bowl of jam, a huge pat of butter, scones —there seemed no end to it. Martha, disguising her dismay at the sight of the three dirty, shabby children, said to Laura, "Come through here to our bathroom. Just wash your hands and faces for now. We'll start baths after tea."

The Colonel was going off to his own quarters when he remembered something.

"Where is the postcard to be sent to your parents, giving the address?"

Laura produced her stamped card from her bag. She had meant to write a word or two on it to stop Mum from worrying, but perhaps some way she could get a stamp in which case she would write tomorrow. She shut out of her mind the fact that she did not know where she would be tomorrow.

The Colonel took the card and saw it was addressed to Mr. & Mrs. Clark, Number 4, Mansfield Road, London, S.E.8., so on the other side under "Have arrived safely," he wrote, "The address is "C/O COLONEL STRANGER STRANGER, SMALL HALL, CHARNBURY, DORSET." Then he gave the card to Elk and told him to take it to the village post office and post it.

Tea passed off pleasantly. Martha, though dismayed at the children's table manners, made no comment. They could snatch at the food as they wanted and stuff as if they had not eaten for a week. The girl was only staying one night and the Colonel had stated, "These evacuee boys will eat with me, Mrs. Elk. They could be with us for years; all this talk of the war being over quickly is poppycock, so right away I shall bring them up as I mean to go on."

The Colonel told Elk to tell his wife that Laura could sleep in his dressing room, but Martha had other ideas. She learned from the children they had shared a bedroom—in fact, a bed—at home, and she planned for the one night they should do the same. All very well for the Colonel to say he didn't mind his dressing room being used for the one night, she thought. He had a mind above nits in the hair and fleas. But she was deeply suspicious as were most of the other foster parents scattered over the country. In this Martha did

Rosie an injustice. By endless use of a small-tooth comb, much paraffin, and baths with carbolic soap her children were vermin free, but Martha was right to be cautious, for many children were not and could easily have passed on nits and fleas on the train.

"There's just the two beds," said Martha to Laura, opening the spare-room door, "but you'll be able to sleep with your little brother just for tonight, won't you?"

Laura was far too overcome to answer. The, to her, huge room with roses on the wallpaper, satin eiderdowns, and thick red curtains and carpet was too beautiful to be real. It belonged to the world of fairy princesses they sometimes were told about in school.

Elk had bathed the two boys in their bath downstairs. Martha had bathed Laura in the Colonel's bathroom. Both Elk and Martha had noticed with surprised pleasure that under their poor patched clothes the three small bodies were remarkably clean.

"We 'ad baths yesterday, Mr. Elk," Andy had protested when told to undress.

"In this house," Elk had said, "the Colonel expects baths every day."

This was so startling an idea that all Andy said was "Cor." Tim was so sleepy after his long day that he said nothing. In fact Elk had to carry him to bed. Martha and Laura did talk a little.

"Is your nightdress in here, dear?" Martha had asked, holding up Laura's paper carrier bag.

Laura took a rather limp little object out of the bag.

"I 'adn't none. Mum got this from the Care Committee lady. It's got flowers on it."

The child was proud of the nightdress so Martha, who

could not admire it, said nothing about it. Instead she asked if the boys had pajamas.

"Tim 'asn't. He has more of a nightshirt but Andy's pajamas is lovely. They're blue. The Care Committee lady give them to Mum—good as new they are."

When the children were in bed and asleep and Martha had tidied and cleaned both bathrooms, she came down to the kitchen to start preparing the Colonel's dinner. Elk was putting china and glass on a tray for laying the dining-room table.

"You can see they come from a poor home," said Martha, "but there's no crime in that, and their parents have done their best to bring them up nicely. Proper little mother that Laura is. Why she even took a rag out of her bag and gave it to little Tim to suck. 'Here's your bobo,' she said, and then to me, 'He'll be asleep in a minute now he's got that,' and he was."

Elk looked worried.

"I thought she was a nice little thing but he's set on giving her back to that Miss Justworthy."

Martha sniffed.

"Her! Beggar on horseback, that's what she is."

There was a pause while they both got on with their work.

Then Martha said, "He thinks a lot of what you say. While you're serving the dinner see if you can put in a word for the girl. D'you know, she saw the boys said their prayers before they went to sleep, not that I think Tim knew he was saying them. Go to Sunday school regular they do, she told me."

"I'll do what I can," Elk agreed, "but I don't hold out much hope. He's taken a proper dislike to that Miss Justworthy."

War

IT HAD BEEN desperately hard to find billeting officers. There was a chief billeting officer in most counties, usually a man, and he was supposed to sort out any special billeting problems as they arose. The chief billeting officer for Charnbury had met Miss Justworthy several times and each time he had sighed, for he looked upon her as a special burden he had to bear. However, on the night of the evacuation, when she rang him up about Laura, he had a clear-cut answer.

"I'm against splitting up families."

"But the Squire says he won't have a girl."

The chief billeting officer thought with affection of the Squire. He could just imagine how Miss Justworthy rubbed him the wrong way.

"We can't make the Squire take her. They're all old in that house—it's good of him to agree to two boys."

"But if he won't have the girl and the family can't be separated, where are they to go?"

Cunningly the chief billeting officer asked, "Have you any

more rooms? How many evacuees have you taken yourself?"

There was a pause and a sort of spluttering noise on the line. Then in a much quieter voice Miss Justworthy said, "I can't see how I can take any evacuees into my home with all the other children to see to."

The chief billeting officer thought about that.

"I'll tell you what I'll do. The Squire's an old friend. I'll ring him tonight and see if I can talk him into taking the three, but if not they all move into your home tomorrow. Agreed?"

The Colonel was half asleep over his good-night whiskey when the telephone rang.

If that is that Justworthy woman, he thought, I'll tell her what I think of her. But when he discovered it was not Miss Justworthy but an old and respected friend he softened.

"It's about your evacuees," the chief billeting officer explained. "I understand your two boys have a sister."

The Colonel blazed into the telephone.

"These amateurs! Can't do a simple job like read what's on the label. Always said I could only take the boys. But that stupid woman . . ."

The chief billeting officer let him run on getting all his anger off his chest. Then he said, "All right. We don't want to split up the family, so I have instructed the Justworthy woman that she is to take your three into her house tomorrow. And if that isn't a fate worse than death I don't know what is."

There was a very long silence after that. Then the Colonel capitulated.

"You win. Wouldn't send a dog to live with that woman, let alone three small children. I don't know how we'll manage but we will."

So the next morning when Martha went to call the children there was a beam on her face.

"It's all settled, dear," she told Laura. "You're staying here with the boys."

The Colonel did not believe in passing on to others what he believed to be his duty. After breakfast, which the children had in the kitchen with the Elks—and a splendid breakfast it was—the Colonel sent for Martha.

"The children have no doubt a lot to learn. It is not right that this burden should fall on you and Elk only, so they will eat breakfast and luncheon with me. I will teach them absolute punctuality and table manners."

Martha thought of the table manners she had seen at tea and breakfast.

"Give them time," she suggested. "In a week or two they'll be easier to work on."

"No," said the Colonel. "We start with luncheon today. Will you see they understand they are to be in the dining room at one o'clock exactly with, of course, washed hands?"

Martha could see troubles ahead but there were things more important than where meals were eaten.

"You'll have to get hold of that Miss Justworthy. The children have almost nothing to wear but what they stand up in and that's only fit for the fire. I washed all their clothes yesterday, but more clothes we must have. There isn't a toothbrush amongst them and, from what Laura says, there's nothing much to come by post."

The Colonel thought this over. He had no faith in any clothes Miss Justworthy could lay her hands on.

"If Elk drove, could you take the children shopping this afternoon and buy what they need?"

"But, sir, you can't. We get only ten shillings and sixpence a week for the first child—that's Laura—and eight shillings and sixpence for each of the others. They aren't yours. It's the government's job to dress them."

The Colonel shook his head.

"If we wait for the government to help we might wait weeks. As I understand you, what our children need they need now. I'll go to the bank this morning and cash a check."

Martha unwillingly agreed to the arrangement but she made a bargain.

"I'll see to getting the clothes but we've got to feel our way. It must be a terrible shock for the children finding themselves living with strangers. So what I think is right, sir, is for the first week I'll keep our three with me for meals and that."

It was to Laura a wonderful afternoon. Never since she was a baby had she owned any new clothes. All she had came from charity handouts or rummage sales. Two night-dresses, a gym slip with two jerseys for school, and a dress to wear at Small Hall—a glorious soft wool frock which, as the assistant pointed out, exactly matched her eyes. For underneath, two of everything. As well, there were shoes with thick soles to wear to school, boots for bad weather, a soft pair of shoes to wear in the house, and something called bedroom slippers to wear in the bedroom. Martha paid for these last out of her own money. She was getting fond of Laura.

Andy thought shopping a bore. He didn't care what he wore or whether he was clean. Elk, however, was instilling into him that these things mattered to the Colonel and that what mattered to the Colonel mattered to them all.

"You disobey him," Elk said, "and I shouldn't wonder if

it was the order of the boot for you three. And then do you know where you'll go?"

"The Tower of London?" Andy suggested.

"Worse nor that," said Elk. "That Miss Justworthy is to give you a home."

Tim was the unluckiest of the family. He was only just five, too small to have the faintest idea what was happening to him. If he had been at home Rosie would have picked him up in her arms and made a fuss of him.

"Now what are you grizzling at?" she would have asked. "You sit on my knee and have a suck of your bobo." But there was no Mum. All he had was a celluloid duck, which was not allowed to come out with him for fear it might be lost. Between meals—which he loved—he had become a whining small boy, and even the nicest person detests a whining child.

The assistant trying clothes on Tim looked at Martha sympathetically.

"You can't please some of these evacuees," she said, "no matter what you do for them."

The next day the children, dressed in their new clothes, were shepherded by the Elks into the drawing room. The Colonel had ordered that the household should hear war declared.

The Colonel said, "The voice you will hear, children, is that of Mr. Neville Chamberlain. He will tell us we are now at war with Germany."

The prime minister came on the air and started his announcement.

"Our dad says he would sooner trust a sewage rat nor him," Andy announced.

The Colonel roared "Silence" in such a voice that even

Andy was cowed. He comforted himself with playing with the little ball Nobby had given him, which was in his pocket.

The announcement over, the prime minister made a speech. He finished by saying, "Now may God bless you all. May he defend the right. It is the evil things we shall be fighting against—brute force, bad faith, injustice, oppression, and persecution—and against them I am certain that the right will prevail."

"Let's hope he's right," said Elk.

"Amen," the Colonel answered. "It's up to us all, however small, to do our best."

Elk looked at the children. Probably the occasion made him feel he was back in the army.

"Left turn," he said, "quick march."

Pocket Money

IT STILL being part of the summer holidays the evacuee children were supposed to have time to settle down and get to know the village children, though many of these, especially those who were the children of farm laborers, had work to do. Those who were free congregated on the village green, but not the Clarks. The Colonel, going back to his own faraway childhood, planned to try to bring them up as he had been brought up himself.

"Can't run to ponies for them," he told Elk, "but you can find them each a garden, and Andy can learn to use a saw and how to clean a car. I enjoyed messing about round the stables when I was his age. The two boys should have cold baths each morning and all three must write home every Sunday. Bed six o'clock, lights out half-past."

"Yes, sir," Elk agreed, privately deciding that for the moment hot baths each night and teeth-cleaning night and morning was all that could be managed.

As it turned out the children up to a point fitted in with the Colonel's plans for them. There was a large garden; it had a big lawn with, at the bottom, a handsome herbaceous border and behind that a hedge hiding a kitchen garden. Mrs. Elk had taken the children to see the garden and had been surprised by Laura's and Tim's reaction.

"Oh!" Laura had gasped at her first sight of the herbaceous border, which was actually at the time looking rather straggly as flower beds will at the beginning of September. "Do all them flars belong to Sir? I mean can 'e pick'm whenever he likes?"

Mrs. Elk knew the children called the Colonel just Sir. It was not very suitable but she had left it to him to find something better.

"Well, he could of course but he never does. All the flower-picking for the house, and sometimes for the church, is left to me."

"Next time flars is picked could I help you? I haven't never picked a flar."

Mrs. Elk could scarcely believe her ears.

"Tell you what," she said after thinking over Laura's words, "suppose I was to teach you, I don't see why you couldn't take on all the flower cutting and arranging for the table and that."

Laura clasped her hands.

"Oh, Mrs. Elk, could I? My mum's fond of flars an' when I write I can tell her. She won't 'alf be pleased."

When shown the place at the end of the garden where their own three gardens would be, Tim had stopped whining and was interested.

"D'you mean I'll 'ave a garden all me own what I don't share with Andy nor Laura?"

"That's right," Mrs. Elk agreed. "Elk's going to dig them tomorrow or next day."

Tim still could not believe it. There had been several plants growing, including mustard and cress, at his nursery school, and the days when he had been allowed to water them had been red-letter days to him.

"I can plant any seeds I like in it?"

"Well, of course, seeds cost money and nothing hasn't been said about pocket money. Not yet it hasn't. But I reckon there'll be some. You ask the Colonel about seeds."

Sunday, the Colonel had decided, was the day when the children had to write home. The first Sunday the Colonel supervised. In his study there was a table and on this he had placed three sheets of notepaper with the address engraved on them. He could well remember the agony of trying to find things to say when he had been forced to write home on Sunday afternoons from his first boarding school, so he tried to help.

"I don't suppose you can write, can you, Tim?"

Laura answered for him.

"No, sir. He only went to the nursery school an' they didn't learn to write there."

Laura looked, the Colonel thought, exactly as little girls ought to look. Under Mrs. Elk's care her hair was beginning to shine and the blue frock exactly matched her eyes. He smiled at her.

"Come along, young Tim," he said in an unusually gentle voice. "You sit on my knee and we'll write your letter together."

They all waited for Tim to scream but, surprisingly, he did not. He just came to the Colonel and climbed on his knee.

"As you and I are going to write this letter together," the Colonel said, "it does not matter that I know what you say.

But ordinarily nobody must ever know what is in somebody else's letter. It is wrong to read somebody else's correspondence."

Tim telling the Colonel what to write down told Nobby and Rosie far more than they got from Laura and Andy's letters. Neither had ever written a letter before and anyway Andy could barely write. He did at last manage in sprawling capitals:

DERE MUM AN DAD IT IS ALRITE ERE LUV ANDY.

Laura did a shade better.

> *Dear Mum and Dad it is a bit of alrite ere there is flars in the garden what Mrs. Elk says what I can pick I have luvly new cloes you did orter to see my blue frock luv Laura.*

The three letters were sealed in one envelope and a day later reached London. Nobby read them out to Rosie. They upset her so much tears dripped down her cheeks. At the end of Tim's dictated letter she said, "You know what it is, if this war lasts long we'll 'ave lost our kids."

Nobby knew what she meant.

"I suppose while things is quiet, no bombs nor that, we could 'ave 'em back."

Rosie shook her head.

"That's what lots are saying and will say more an' more as Christmas comes along. But our street warden"—by then the men and women with W on their tin hats were known as wardens—"said when it starts it will start sudden and there won't be the same evacuation then. He said it's downright wicked to bring them back."

"He doesn't 'ave kids so 'e doesn't know what the 'ouse is like without 'em," said Nobby.

"No," Rosie choked back a sob. " 'E doesn't know."

Tim's letter home had said many things. "There is smashing food here but no fish and chips. Sir makes us have a bath every day and clean our teeth twice. We have new clothes. I am going to have a garden all my own and if we get pocket money I shall buy seeds and if they come up I shall send you some."

"I don't like my kids bein' beholden to this Colonel," said Nobby. "Of course 'e wrote Tim's letter but I reckon in 'is own way our Tim said what was to be put down. I wish I could manage this pocket money."

Since war had been declared there was rather more work about. Rosie and Nobby looked around them. The house without the children looked exceptionally derelict.

"We did ought've got the things out of pawn before the children comes 'ome," Rosie said. "I mean, so the 'ouse is more like what they're livin' in now."

Nobby thought for a bit.

"If I was to cut out smoking I could manage sixpence a week for each."

Rosie hated Nobby to go without anything.

"I don't like you to give anythin' up. You don't know 'ow things will be in the navy."

"That may not 'appen for months," Nobby pointed out. "No, I reckon sixpence a week it is, an' I'll write to that Colonel to say so. Pass over that card with 'is name on so I spells it right."

Two days later the Colonel received a letter written on a page torn from a lined schoolbook.

Dear Sir me and the wife don't like not to do nothing for our kids so please find P.O. for one shilling and sixpence this is spendin money and will come each week I am no good at the writin but the wife an me cant thank you proper for all yore doing finding you as it leaves me at present Nobby Clark.

Laura, glowing with pleasure, was picking flowers in the herbaceous border and Andy was helping Elk clean the car when the letter arrived, so the Colonel read it to Tim, whom he found gazing at the piece of earth which would one day be his garden.

"I've got to go to the post office to cash this," said the Colonel, showing Tim the postal order. Then he felt in his pocket, "But here's your sixpence."

"When could I buy seeds?" Tim asked.

The Colonel thought back to his own first garden. It had had one very showy plant in it. It had been a marguerite. The sixpence would not pay for that but perhaps he could help.

"Tell you what, Tim, after luncheon we'll go down to the village and see what we can find. Shouldn't wonder if we weren't being told to grow food pretty soon. So how about you making a start on some radishes?"

Fitting In

WHEN THE evacuees had first arrived in Charnbury, since the school was not big enough to take the extra children, the local children had gone to school in the morning and the evacuees in the afternoon. Then, as September faded into October and October into November and there were still no bombs, the evacuees began to vanish, so the Clarks could attend school morning and afternoon. It was natural that families wanted their children back. Toys in the shop windows and the beginning of decorations made Christmas seem close. Nor had all the children been as happily billeted as the Clarks. There were some who knew their foster parents did not want them, some who found country rules for good behavior irksome, and some who did not like living in the country. Anyway, whatever the reason in spite of advice from everybody to stay put, slowly the evacuees departed from Charnbury until there were under twenty left, including the Clarks.

It was hard for parents to believe the oft-repeated warning that sooner or later the bombs would fall. Next time there would be no official evacuation scheme and, it could be, no home willing to take in evacuees. Nor did all the foster parents bother with warnings. They made no bones about being thankful to see the backs of their unwanted guests. These were foster parents who, ever since the evacuees had arrived, bombarded Miss Justworthy with demands for clothes and with claims for damage done to furniture, carpets, and bed linen. The same foster parents gathered in the post office to tell each other of the latest piece of scandalous behavior performed by their evacuees.

Because of traffic on the road, Elk usually took Laura and Andy to school and fetched them home at dinnertime and collected them again at 3:30.

While this was going on the Colonel did what he could to amuse Tim, who was too small for school. Gradually they had become friends. The friendship was first based on Tim's garden.

"You don't want to go too much for seeds this time of year," the Colonel explained. "This is bulb planting time."

"Can I get bulbs with my sixpence?" Tim had asked.

"Elk orders the bulbs. You tell him how many sixpences you want to spend. I should go for crocuses and snowdrops— the early things. Then when they're finished you can start helping to grow food."

In spite of too much watering and far too much feeling to see how they were getting on, Tim's radishes had been an enormous success. They were eaten for kitchen tea, and everyone thought them perfect. One was taken into the drawing room for the Colonel's tea, and Elk brought back a message that the Colonel had never tasted better. Tim felt swollen with pride.

There was no pride for Laura and Andy in their gardens.

Andy, following Elk round, found many more interesting things to do than gardening, which he thought a bore.

"I don't want a garden," he told Elk. "You tell Sir and he can give mine to Tim."

Laura was not willing to part with her garden. Somewhere in her head an idea swam about, in which she had a garden as full of flowers as Elk's seed catalogue. Only somehow she did not see herself digging and planting. Laura, like Andy, was finding too many other nice things to do. Martha had been appalled at how little Laura knew of what she called "womanly things." The children had not been in the house a week before she discovered that Laura could not sew. There was a stitch wanted in her gym slip.

"My work basket's on the shelf there," Martha said. "There's a reel of navy cotton. See you fix the cotton in its slot when you've finished. I can't abide tangles of cotton in my work basket."

Laura had fetched the work basket. It was, though she did not know it, a model of what a work basket should look like. Reels of cotton in a neat row. A needle book full of every size of needle. A leather case containing three different sizes of scissors. In the lid were loops for thimbles.

Laura's admiring gaze at the basket had been interrupted by Martha.

"Come on, Laura, a work basket is not to be looked at but to be used."

Rosie owned a needle. It was stuck for safety into an old calendar. There had, too, been reels of cotton, one black, one white, on the ledge above the fireplace. When something had to be mended or a button sewn on Rosie would say, "Give it here." Then when the job was finished she would bite off the end of cotton and put both the needle and the cotton reel back in their places. "Don't you kids never touch them," she would say, "for there's no more where they come from."

Now Laura looked at Martha.

"I never done no sewin'. I wasn't in the class what learned it at the school."

"Well, I'll teach you then," Martha said, disguising not for the first time what she thought of Rosie. "Now first we'll have to put some paper in the smallest thimble to make it fit your finger."

After that, sewing lessons became fairly regular. To encourage Laura, Martha said, "How about making a Christmas present for your mother? How about a nice handkerchief? But first you'll have to practice hemming."

So every day after tea Laura struggled to thread needles and to sew.

"You put me in mind of me when I was a little girl," Martha told her. "My first piece of sewing was a handkerchief for my mother. I embroidered her initial in the corner."

Laura could not see a place for a handkerchief with an initial on it in Rosie's house. Martha had never known unemployment, nor having no money, nor a world where there was no iron to look after pretty handkerchiefs. Martha only knew having lots of everything, including a place called a larder, which was always full of food. Where nobody ran out with a few pence to buy the next meal. Martha did not know a world where most days the next meal, when it came, was not enough.

Laura was the only member of the family who thought about being an evacuee. Andy accepted everything that happened to him as a right, except those things he actively disliked, and then he would feel cross and tell Laura about it.

Tim was too small to think much, but though he did not know it he had become a different child from the whining little scrap who had left London on the first of September. He was looking different; good regular meals and long nights in bed had filled him out, and he felt fine. If, as sometimes happened, he whined in his old way for what he wanted, the Colonel would say in a fierce voice, "Stop that noise and ask politely for what you want and maybe you'll get it."

There really were only two things about living in Small Hall that Andy disliked. The first was bedtime. This was something which made him see red. He told Elk how he felt one evening when Elk was supervising his bath.

"Colonel's orders," Elk had replied briskly. "No one don't argue with him."

"But I do!" Andy had shouted. "All the other boys are out playing. Why should I be in bed?"

"Ask the Colonel," Elk said. "And you got a pair of ears that want washing same as everything else."

That was in September and, ever since, Andy had been trying to ask the Colonel only somehow he couldn't. Sir was not the type to argue with. Instead, when the spare room door was shut and the lights put out, he would grumble to Laura.

"Why can't I go out to play like I always done? I didn't never go to bed not before I felt like it at 'ome."

"The Colonel says children need twelve hours' sleep," Laura would explain. "When we go 'ome after the war you can go to bed when you likes. It's different 'ere."

It would have been possible for Andy to get out of the window. There was a handy tree for him to climb down. He never did, and Laura knew he never would. To do anything as bad as that in Sir's house was unthinkable. The other trouble was luncheon. Because of school hours the children were still having breakfast in the kitchen, but they took lunch with the Colonel and it was an ordeal. Tim came off best for his food was cut up for him. Laura and Andy had to eat properly: "Knife in the right hand, fork in the left." "Never speak when you have food in your mouth." "You have a table napkin so don't use the back of your hand to wipe your mouths." "Keep your elbows off the table." "You have a spoon for your pudding so do not use your fingers." It was a nightmare. Longingly Laura and Andy would remember fish and chips eaten, soaked in vinegar, out of a piece of newspaper.

"Of all the thin's we 'ave to learn in this 'ouse eatin's the worst," Andy would explode.

Laura had to agree with him.

The war was scarcely mentioned in front of the children. At school they were told about the sinking of the P. & O. liner *Rawalpindi*, to show how brave British sailors were. After being told the story they all sang "Eternal Father Strong to Save" followed by "God Save the King." This made a pleasant change in school routine so the children wished it could happen more often. It did not, however, bring the war nearer, for few of the children had seen the sea, let alone a big ship.

A tremendous effort was made in Charnbury to give the evacuees a Christmas party. As well, there was Christmas in their foster homes, complete at Small Hall with filled stockings, a Christmas tree and turkey and plum pudding. Yet somehow it just wasn't like Christmas for anybody, and many grownups and even some of the children were glad when it was over. They were glad, too, when it was the New Year and they could say good-by to what was called the "bore" war and call out "Happy New Year, happy 1940."

Though the children were not told, the Colonel made a great effort to get Nobby and Rosie down for a night before Nobby joined the navy. It was Nobby and Rosie who, after much talk, decided against it.

"We wouldn't fit in like," Rosie told Nobby, "nor I 'aven't the clothes to go. Besides, we don't want to unsettle the kids. They're used to funny ways like going to bed at six."

Nobby sorrowfully agreed. Then he brightened up.

"When I'm in me uniform it will be different. The kids'll be proud of me then."

"And after you're gone, if I'm working in a factory, I can buy clothes," Rosie pointed out. "I'd fancy goin' for the day on a Whitsun Bank 'oliday."

The year began by being bitterly cold, so cold everything froze. It was so cold a party of men from the farms went twice a week by sledge to the nearest town for bread and other necessities. To the evacuees this was wildly exciting. All their lives there had been shops round the corner. They had, of course, known the country was different from London, but so different that you could be completely cut off was outside anything they had imagined. During this period all the evacuee children learned the exquisite pleasure of riding down a steep hill on a tin tray.

The cold weather was followed by a most glorious spring. It was so beautiful that Laura tried to tell Nobby and Rosie about it. In her Sunday letter she wrote: "Here the spring comes up like a carpet all made of flowers."

Other things happened that spring beside flowers coming up. Early in May, Elk came into the garden where the children were playing and announced in his army voice that the Colonel wanted everybody to come into his study. The Colonel always did look like a soldier but that day he had an added look; it was as if he was made of courage.

"Today," he said, "Germany has invaded Holland, Belgium, and Luxembourg by both land and air. They have all appealed to us for help. Mr. Chamberlain is no longer our prime minister. We have now a new name to remember. It is Mr. Winston Churchill. Now say that name after me."

They all repeated it solemnly. "Our new prime minister is Mr. Winston Churchill."

Elk wished he had support from a bugler or a drum but he gave his usual command sounding even more military than usual: "Left turn, quick march."

In the weeks that followed, life became queer in Charnbury. The grownups talked very little and even the children were quieter.

"I feel like I did before we were evacuated," Laura told Andy. "Everybody whispers as if they didn't want us children to hear."

This was of course true. In spite of brave writing in the newspapers and brave talk on the wireless, the people of Charnbury were no more fooled than the rest of the country. Whatever was happening in France the British were not advancing. But there was no panic—in fact a lot of common sense was shown.

"We've been in worse fixes before." "You wait till Winston Churchill speaks. He'll tell us what us should be doing."

When Winston Churchill did speak the Colonel made a great occasion of it. In his study over the mantelpiece he hung a Union Jack. On the wall there was a map with little flags stuck in it.

"Today," the Colonel said, "is a day we shall remember all our lives. Our army is cut off here." He laid his hand on the piece of France marked Dunkirk. "There were far too many men for our naval ships to carry so everybody who had even a little rowing boat was asked to help. And they came. All the tugs from the Thames—you children will have seen those—pleasure steamers, motor boats, drifters, tramps, trawlers, anything that could float. Mr. Churchill told the House of Commons that he feared that only about twenty to thirty thousand men could be rescued; instead over 335,000 men, French and British, are now safe on this island."

The Colonel had to pause there. For a second Laura was afraid he was going to cry, but of course he didn't—colonels don't. When he spoke again it was in a different voice.

"Now a new life faces us all. It will mean doing without things, even for you little children; but I know, and Mr. Churchill knows, you will be glad to help."

Before Elk could get out, "Left turn," Andy said, "Our dad won't 'alf be mad 'e wasn't on one of them little boats."

The Colonel smiled. "He will, Andy, he certainly will, and so say all of us."

In spite of what the Colonel had told them nothing different, as far as the children could see, happened for weeks and weeks. From the children's viewpoint the most important thing that occurred was Laura's tenth birthday. There was rationing, so Mrs. Elk told them, and she fussed about using eggs and sugar, but on the great day she had managed a splendid cake, and if it was a little smaller than had been the one for Andy's eighth birthday in February, only she noticed.

Nobby was now in the merchant navy. Not even Rosie knew where he was or what ship he was on because the sea, so the Colonel told the children, was full of German sub-marines that would like to find out about sailings of British ships so that they could try and sink them. Not, of course, that they could but they might try.

Rosie was now working in a factory. She was lucky that on the next machine to her was an educated girl who wrote letters for her during the dinner hour. Because of this girl, whose name was Beaty, the whole house knew more about Rosie than they had known since the children arrived. Beaty did not alter Rosie's style; but she spelled the words properly and put in punctuation when it was needed.

Beaty's first letter said:

> *Dear kids,*
>
> *Your dad is a sailor now. I don't know where but he looks smashing in his sailor suit and would you believe it after a few weeks' training he would not let me wash his clothes. 'I do my own dhoby-ing now.' He said dhobying is what the navy calls washing. He said you never can tell how things will turn out but some day he might surprise you all by dropping in. I don't half wish he would drop in here.*
>
> *You was told about how our boys was got back from Dunkirk. Well, when they come home they left all their stuff behind like guns and tanks and that, so thousands more was needed and what I am doing is helping to make them.*
>
> *Luv Mum.*

Afterwards Laura looked upon her tenth birthday as a sort of landmark. It was after it that everything in Charnbury started to change. Sir and Elk became soldiers, both joined the Local Defense Volunteers, which was later called the Home Guard. They all wore armbands with L.D.V. painted on them. The Colonel was put in charge of the Charnbury branch and in the evenings, on Saturday afternoons and all day on Sunday, he and Elk marched off with groups of men and taught them to drill. This, of course, meant that every boy in Charnbury, including Andy and Tim, wanted to be soldiers too. Even the real soldiers hadn't many weapons, and of course the Local Defense Volunteers had none, so they used broomsticks as pretend rifles. This was splendid for the boys, who used broomsticks, too, and got dreadfully in the way drilling behind the men and imitating the worst drillers. The Colonel was not having his Defense Volunteers made fun of, but he believed in everybody's helping and he had the perfect job for the boys. So he went to see them in school. The whole school was lined up to hear what he had to say.

"Because of the war," he told them, "special powers have been given to me and to Mr. Sift." Mr. Sift was the local Air Raid Warden. "So we could, if we so wished, order you boys who are making a nuisance of yourselves to stay in your homes during the hours when the Defense Volunteers are on parade. However, as things have turned out, we now have special work for all you boys. It is expected that the Germans, by boat and by air, will attempt to land on this island. They will not of course succeed. You will in the next day or so see our roads being blocked. You will see piles of bottles filled with homemade explosive being collected. These will be called Molotov cocktails. They are for throwing at tanks. But what you have to think about is Germans landing by air. They won't look like soldiers. They may be dressed as women—even as nuns. Each will have a map and each will try to find his way probably to London.

"Now for your work. We want all you local boys who know the roads and the footpaths to make up teams with our visitors from London to see to it that no German gets any help from road signs. Turn the signs round so they point the wrong way. Lead the enemy on wild goose chases, but best of all lead them to us of the Defense Volunteers. We'll soon have them under lock and key."

No boy who took part in the great orgy of messing up the road signs ever forgot it. There was, too, another side to the business and that concerned the girls as well. It was practicing giving the wrong directions by mouth. Frustrated lorry, or truck, drivers carrying urgent war supplies were driven almost to hysteria by children who, being asked if this was the road to London, either said they didn't know or pointed back down the road up which the lorry driver had just driven.

Andy and Tim were valuable members of the boy teams. Tim was particularly useful, for he looked so young that it was worth putting him at vantage points where Germans might land. More often than not it was Tim who told the helpless lorry drivers, "You can't get to London this way. There's a turning three miles back."

To Laura it was like being back in 1939. She was afraid and had no one to talk to about it. To be afraid was now a shocking disgrace, something nobody admitted to being. Look at Andy and Tim. Far from being afraid they prayed every night that the Germans would come. Oh God, please send the Germans soon! But at the thought of Germans dropping out of the sky Laura's inside seemed to turn over. Then there was Dad. Sir could say what he liked, but ships did get sunk. She had heard children talking about it at school.

Then there was the battle in the air, which raged all that summer. Charnbury was off the main route but most days there was a dog fight in the distance, so everyone knew the clatter clatter of airplanes firing at each other. Everybody else seemed to stand and stare at the sky, full of hope that they would see a German plane come down. Laura appeared to be the only person who was afraid an airplane might fall on her.

That summer was forever remembered by Laura, not only because she was afraid but for the strange accompaniment to her frightened thoughts while lying in bed—the tinkle, tinkle from the kitchen where Sir and the Elks filled baskets with their homemade Molotov cocktails.

Mushrooms

THE NEXT thing that happened was the arrival of more evacuees. This time not in expected groups but in straggling parties of all ages. The people of Charnbury were almost sorry for Miss Justworthy. She had such a mixed collection begging to be housed and such resistant householders to deal with. For now it wasn't a matter of squeezing in an extra girl like Laura. It was finding homes for very old men and women and mothers expecting babies.

"You'll have to move into the Colonel's dressing room," Mrs. Elk told Laura. "If that Justworthy woman gets her foot in the door and sees the bed is not used she'll land goodness knows who on us."

Inside the house, by the Colonel's order, why the new evacuees were there was never mentioned, but of course the children heard the truth at school. London was being bombed. The stories told were grisly and often exaggerated but somehow it seemed not to concern them. None of the children had ever been bombed so they could not imagine what it was like.

It was when Laura was telling Tim that she was going to sleep in Sir's dressing room that she realized how long a time they had lived in Charnbury. She knew, of course, they had been living in Small Hall for over a year but she had not noticed how much they had grown up. When she remembered the whining, crying five-year-old who sucked a bobo, it seemed impossible he had ever been Tim. Now he was a tough six-year-old who only said when he heard about the changed sleeping arrangements, "O.K. I'll be glad of more room."

Mrs. Elk was thankful it had all been arranged, for the very next day Miss Justworthy arrived on the doorstep with a frail little old lady.

"Could you help, Mrs. Elk?" Miss Justworthy implored.

"I wouldn't trouble anybody, dear," said the old lady, "but my room was blowed away."

Mrs. Elk made sympathetic noises.

"Oh dear! I wish I could help. But every bed is full. Did you lose everything? I mean perhaps we could help with furniture or that."

The old lady quietly turned to go.

"No, nothing to matter. All I had really was my budgie bird. He was found dead in his cage. I couldn't take him to the shelter for he would talk. Lovely talker was my budgie."

It was a Saturday morning, so the children were not in school and had heard the conversation. They watched Miss Justworthy putting the old lady into her car. The boys were not really interested but there was something about Mrs. Elk's back which made Laura follow her into the kitchen. There she found she was crying. Laura did not know what to do, for Mrs. Elk was the last person to cry.

"I could go back with Tim," she suggested. "Then there'd

be room for the old lady."

Mrs. Elk just sat with tears, which she made no effort to wipe away, dripping down her cheeks.

"I know, dear. It's not that. It's the Colonel. He's not well and one more thing might be too much."

Seeing the Colonel every day, Laura had not thought about him as being either ill or well—he was just there. But now she remembered something.

"He does walk slow."

Mrs. Elk nodded.

"He hasn't the breath to go faster. He shouldn't be out in all weathers with his Home Guard; it isn't right. All last Sunday crawling amongst wet cabbages."

The Home Guard was now a recognized part of Charnbury's life. The broomsticks had gone and every man had a rifle. Behind every kitchen door hung a khaki overcoat. Charnbury being mainly agricultural, only a few men had left to join the forces; the rest grew food and were ready when called on to fight the Germans. It was a way of life. Laura could not imagine the Colonel not being in command.

"He wouldn't like being stopped doing it."

Mrs. Elk nodded.

"Nobody could stop him. All I can do is see he rests all he can and he won't do that if I take in another evacuee. He'll keep feeling he ought to be doing something for them."

To Laura's grief the herbaceous border was being dug up and planted with vegetables. Elk was doing the job, but Laura had watched the Colonel helping.

"I'll tell Andy and Tim. We could help Mr. Elk dig up the border."

Mrs. Elk seemed to pull herself together and want to get back to normal.

"Yes, dear, you do that." She made a real effort. "Tell you what. After last night's rain I know a place where there could be mushrooms. How about you coming with me to look? I could give the Colonel mushrooms on toast for his dinner. He's very partial to them."

So that afternoon, carrying a basket, Mrs. Elk and Laura set off for the mushroom field. It was some way from the house, but it was a lovely afternoon, the hedges glowing with red and purple berries overlaid with a cloud of traveler's-joy. Only one thing spoiled Laura's pleasure; it was the hum of an airplane somewhere in the sky. The period when there were air battles all day long had ceased, and now they seldom heard planes until the evenings. Then they often heard the roar as waves of attackers went over to bomb some town.

Mrs. Elk heard the plane too.

"Whoever that is sounds lost. Probably comes from one of these places they are training them to fly."

There were mushrooms, large and in splendid condition. Mrs. Elk carefully taught Laura how to know them from toadstools.

"They come up in rings. See. Follow the ring around and you'll often find a small one no bigger than a button. Now, when you peel them see the skin peels back easy like this. The stalk is never spindly but solid like. Mind you never eat mushrooms, not without you've shown them to me first."

Mrs. Elk broke off there and stood gaping at the sky. The airplane had stopped humming and was coming down nose first, evidently preparing to crash. Beside it floated a parachute.

The airplane crashed into a wood, where it exploded, and some trees caught fire. The parachute came down in the mushroom field. Out of it tumbled a young fair-haired boy in German uniform. Mrs. Elk acted as though she had been meeting German parachutists every day.

"Stay there," she told Laura, and then walked steadily toward the boy. She called out, "Give me your gun."

To Laura's amazement the boy did as he was told and then, also as ordered, put his hands on his head. Then, with Mrs. Elk poking him in the back with his revolver, they came back to Laura. Laura was so scared she had nearly lost her voice.

"Are you going to shoot 'im?"

Mrs. Elk said calmly, "Not if he behaves himself."

"Should I go and look for somebody?" Laura suggested.

Mrs. Elk might have arrested German airmen all her life.

"No, dear. That plane crashing will bring them all. The Colonel, Mr. Elk, and all the Home Guard. The warden, too, shouldn't wonder."

"What are you going to do with him? I mean till someone comes."

"You pick up the mushrooms and lead the way to the road. They'll see us there. I'll give him a push to see he follows you."

On the road, which they reached safely, Laura remembered what she had been taught. She turned to the airman and pointed back to Charnbury.

"London," she said.

The boy smiled and shook his head.

"Nein." Then, gesturing with his head, he pointed out the way to London.

Almost at once in every kind of vehicle the whole male population of Charnbury arrived. Mrs. Elk gave the revolver to the Colonel.

"He got out of a parachute. Laura and I saw him come

down. So we caught him for you."

"Did he try and run for it?" one of the Home Guard asked.

Mrs. Elk looked scornful.

"Where could he run to?" Then she turned back to the Colonel. "If you could bring him to the house, sir, while you telephone for the police and that, I could give him a cup of tea."

Laura's and Martha's German was talked about for weeks. A photographer came from a newspaper and took their photographs. It was the women who kept the story going. If at the end of an evening's drill the men of the Home Guard went into the pub for a drink and were delayed getting home, almost always they were met with, "We was pretty troubled about you. We was planning to send out Laura and Mrs. Elk in case you had come across a German."

Now that Mrs. Elk had pointed it out, Laura began to notice that the Colonel was not as good at getting about as he had been. She told the boys what Mrs. Elk had said.

"So, now that Mr. Elk is planting vegetables in the big bed could you help, so Sir doesn't have to?"

"You do it, Tim," Andy suggested. "You like gardens. I'm cutting up logs for the fires and heaps of other things."

"I think we'll all have to help so Sir can see he isn't needed."

Elk did not receive the children's offer of help graciously.

"You leave me be," he growled. "I know where I want things put. If you got time, Laura, you lend Mrs. Elk a hand; she can do with it. You stick to your woodcutting, Andy. Looks like we'll soon be needing fires. I got some plants for you, Tim, so if you wants to dig—dig up your own garden."

But perhaps the Colonel knew Mrs. Elk was worried. Anyway he gave up gardening.

Because Mrs. Elk seldom talked about it and was a splendid manager the children did not think much about rationing, but they heard a lot about it in Beaty's letters from Rosie.

"I hope things are better for you in the country than for us in London. Living alone I don't get enough on my ration book to keep a sparrow going. But in the shelter of a night there's a canteen comes round and I can buy buns and that, buns is very filling."

That November when London was being bombed every night the Colonel wrote to Rosie.

> *Dear Mrs. Clark,*
> *It is now over a year since you saw your children. They are I think looking well and we are all fond of them. Would it be possible for you to come here for Christmas Day? I do not know exactly what accommodation we can offer but we will do the best we can, and having you will be a delight to the children.*
> *Yours sincerely,*
> *Launcelot Stranger Stranger.*

The Colonel did not tell the children he had written to Rosie, but of course he told the Elks.

"Just for Christmas, Laura can move back with the boys. We must make a great effort to make this a splendid Christmas. We must not, of course, accept more than our share of what is going, but I think I know where I might obtain a goose."

Beaty wrote an answer for Rosie four days later.

> *Dear Sir,*
>   *I am that excited I can't sleep at nights which is funny for I find the guns generally rocks me off. The factory is not closing but mothers with evacuated children can take Christmas Day off to spend with them. I will come early Christmas morning. Tell the kids I am already shopping in my dinner time. I have written to tell their dad but I don't of course know where he is.*
> *Yours faithfully,*
> *Rosie Clark.*

home from school. Their reaction was unexpected. They
    The Colonel told the children the news when they came could none of them imagine their mother in Charnbury. She was home, she was London.

"She hasn't never been in a place like this," said Andy.

Laura struggled to picture Mum sitting at the dining-room table with the Colonel, learning all those tiresome eating rules.

"We 'aven't got no dining room at 'ome," she said.

By degrees, imitating the Colonel, the children were beginning to learn not to drop all their aitches. Usually he would correct them gently, saying home starts with an aitch, or something like that. This time he said nothing for it was clear he had startled the children.

"What about you, Tim?" he asked. "Won't it be exciting to see your mother again?"

Tim struggled to remember. But over a year is a long time if you were only just five when it started. Then he remembered the good-by presents.

"I don't want another duck," he said.

Of course these first reactions didn't last. Soon, talking together, the children got excited. Mum was coming for one whole day. Her war work wouldn't spare her for longer. Everything must be crammed into the one day.

"I wish it wasn't winter," Laura mourned. "Though we haven't flowers no more she'd have loved to see the blue-bells."

Andy was good at games.

"I wish she could see me play football," he said. "But I could put on me boots so she could see them."

Laura thought of her appearance.

"I'm glad I've still got my blue frock. I've told her about that ever so often."

The Elks suggested homemade presents. Mrs. Elk, doing most of the work herself, taught Laura to make her mother a pair of gloves. There was no wool to be bought in the village shop but she unpicked an old navy jersey and they used the wool from that.

Elk, who was a good carpenter, showed Andy how to make a stand for a plant. Andy thought it beautiful and forgot there had been no plants in his home to stand on it.

Tim made his Christmas present at school: cut-out pic tures and stars were stuck on a cardboard folder and a piece of blotting paper was folded inside.

As Christmas Day drew nearer plans were completed. Gas was rationed so the car could be used only for Home Guard work. This was a grief to the children.

"Mum wouldn't half 'ave liked to have been driven in our car."

Elk had winked.

"Don't say a word but I'm working on it. I got a petrol coupon put away the Colonel don't know about."

"But he'll see the car," Andy said.

Elk shook his head.

"Your mum's train gets in while he's in church. You're to miss church just the once."

From the kitchen came glorious smells. Food was getting very scarce, even in the country, where you could sometimes come by a rabbit.

"But for the Colonel we could do much better," Mrs. Elk would say, "but he just won't have anything come into this house that is more than our share. Still, Christmas is Christmas and if his Home Guard like to show a bit of Christmas spirit by giving us two eggs or even a pound of sausages, Colonel or no Colonel I'm not saying no."

The children, accustomed now to very plain food, found their mouths watering as they smelled the lovely food being locked away for Christmas Day.

"It's to be 'oped Mum's hungry," said Andy. "Mr. Elk says there is enough now for four mums."

The week before Christmas there was a special parade of the Home Guard. It was to finish with a glass of beer in the local pub. The Colonel, with his back like a ramrod even if his steps were slow, started to address his men.

"It is my proud duty . . ." he said.

Then he fell in a heap onto the ground. A doctor was called, but he was dead.

After the Colonel

T H E   N E X T few days were like being in a tunnel in a train, a sort of lasting blackness. Because everybody was sad and wanted to help, the children were continually being asked out to meals. Now that the evacuees from bombed London had been squeezed in on top of the remaining original evacuees the children were going to school only for half-days. To help the Elks the villagers invited the children for the rest of the day.

"Don't you worry, Mrs. Elk. With extra potatoes what we have will do."

The children hated being pushed around. They were sad about the Colonel and missed him very much, but there seemed to them no reason why things should not go on as usual.

"I don't see why it helps Mrs. Elk not to cook our dinner," Andy grumbled. "She's cooking theirs."

"She thinks it's rude to say we won't come when people are so kind," said Laura. "She told me so."

After much thought Mrs. Elk had written to Rosie.

"I am grieved to inform you that the Colonel is dead. He was taken very sudden at a Home Guard parade. Changes will have to be made but not before Christmas so please do come as arranged."

To this came no reply at all. Then two days before Christmas there was a Christmas card from Beaty. It said:

> *Sorry your mum can't come for Christmas. She will be ever so disappointed.*
>
> *Beaty.*

In the privacy of her bedroom Martha let herself go.

"Of all the inconsiderate women! And I wrote her ever such a nice letter. After all the trouble I've taken to have things nice."

Elk said, "I reckon she is meaning to help. She'll know we shan't feel like Christmas this year."

Of course the children were disappointed their mother was not coming after all. But they posted her their presents. What was surprising was that there was no parcel for them. Last year there had been a parcel with presents for everybody, including the Colonel and the Elks; very simple presents, for their father had not been working full time—but presents. Now there was nothing at all. Yet in their mother's letters written by Beaty she had said each week she was buying presents to bring.

"Not to worry," said Mrs. Elk. "Maybe she's planning to come for the New Year."

The children had a grand Christmas: bulging stockings, a Christmas tree, and the most splendid food. And even the Elks stopped being sad that day and Mr. Elk dressed up and sang army songs with choruses.

But after Christmas things grew darker and more like a tunnel than ever. People kept coming to the house and talking to the Elks behind closed doors and often a man seemed to be there measuring things. The New Year passed and not only did their mother not come but she didn't write. The children, of course, wrote to her each Sunday but they could not write to Beaty for they didn't know her surname.

"I don't like it," Martha told Elk. "Even when she wrote herself she always wrote. It's so funny just stopping writing like that. I do hope nothing's happened to her."

Elk had thought this matter out.

"I don't think anything could have. The children came from their school and I reckon the school would be told if anything was wrong."

It was not until February that the children were told there were to be changes. As often happens, February was being a beastly month. The weather was wretched and, though the children did not know much about the war, the news was terrible. The U-boats were sinking even larger numbers of ships and this meant food was growing scarcer every day. With the help of home-grown vegetables and the occasional rabbit or odd game bird, country people did better than town people. This did not mean they got more rations, for men from the Ministry of Food kept a sharp eye on farms. It was not easy to hide even a piglet from their unexpected visits and sharp eyes, but they had more at hand to help out.

That winter in Small Hall they all sat in the dining room. Since the Colonel's death, it had been turned into a general living room, for they had not the fuel for more than one fire. It was also a means of having the children where the Elks could lay hands on them. For at that time even Charnbury had air-raid warnings and once, to the immense pride

of every child in the village, they had a bomb. It only fell
on a plowed field, but "our crater" was the village treasure.
Now other places than London were bombed occasionally
so most country areas knew the sound of planes overhead.
Sometimes a lost plane would drop its bombs just anywhere
before making for home. When the siren—which the new
evacuees called the sireen—wailed, the Elks hustled the
children into the cellar, where they sat rolled up in rugs
waiting for the siren to signal the All Clear.

It was one teatime that Elk said, "I got to tell you three a
piece of bad news. We've got to leave this house."

Small Hall, even without the Colonel, was home. The
children were shocked.

"Where we going then?" Andy asked.

"I got potatoes not dug up yet in my garden," Tim reminded Elk.

Laura couldn't say anything. Move. Move where? Clear
as anything she could hear her mother's voice at the station
a year and a half ago.

"See you look after the boys, Laura. They're in your
charge now."

Elk went on.

"The Colonel knew this place would be bigger than
what we'd want so he left me the cottage. You know it, up
by Gedge's farm."

Of course the children knew the cottage. Gedge was the
biggest farmer thereabouts. It was he who had bought the
Colonel's land.

Andy said, "But there's the land girls in it."

Everybody knew Mr. Gedge's four bouncing land girls.

"That's just it," Elk agreed. "They can't be moved on
account they are part of the war effort."

"So," Mrs. Elk broke in, "just while the war lasts we're going to live along with Mr. Elk's mother. She's over ninety and shouldn't be alone."

At last Laura found her voice.

"But what's happening to this house?"

"It's been left to a relative of the Colonel but he's in the army somewhere," Mrs. Elk explained, "and meanwhile this house is requisitioned. That means taken over without a 'by your leave.' It's to be a hospital for all the girls evacuated to these parts to have their babies."

Laura tried again.

"Then where are we going?"

Mrs. Elk had dreaded that question. If it had been in any way possible she would have taken the children with her. But it was impossible. Elk's mother could no longer climb stairs so she spent her days in her living room–kitchen. Upstairs there was only the bedroom, for the cottage was part of what had been a larger building. Mrs. Elk wrestled with a lump in her throat.

"Miss Justworthy is making arrangements for you."

The children loved the Elks. Even more than the Colonel they had made Small Hall home. None of them could believe that such friends would give them to Miss Justworthy. It would be like throwing them to a lioness. Like everyone else in the village they knew that every bedroom was full— often overfull. There was only one place with an empty room and that was Miss Justworthy's house.

"That old lady, the one whose bird was killed by a bomb, the one they took in at the pub, they say she'll not last. Could we go there like?" Andy suggested.

Laura shook her head.

"Someone in the Women's Institute got her a new budgie

bird. She's got better since."

"There must be somewhere else than Miss Justworthy." Andy was almost shouting. "There must."

"How long before you go?" Laura asked the Elks.

"Monday," said Elk. "The Colonel left me the car and I've been given petrol for the move."

Monday was only a week away. It was clear even to Andy that nothing could be done. The Elks were going, the house was going, there was only Miss Justworthy. Andy almost never cried but he burst into tears then as did Tim and Laura. The children were still sobbing when at six o'clock— nobody had interfered with the Colonel's rules—the Elks gave them their baths and put them into bed.

Laura, in the Colonel's dressing room, seemed to have been in bed for hours when she felt a tug on the bedclothes.

Andy whispered, "Let me in."

Laura made room for him.

"What's the matter?"

Andy spoke in a whisper.

"I'm not going to that Justworthy."

"There's nowhere else."

"I know. All the same, I ain't goin'. The last lot she took she made do all the work and she didn't give 'em enough to eat. They say she feeds 'em on cat food."

"But if there's nowhere else," Laura objected, "we'll have to go. Maybe it won't be for long. Someone might leave or die and she won't want us no more'n we want 'er."

"I ain't goin' to 'er," Andy said.

"Then where?" Laura asked.

" 'Ome. There's always lorries driving on the road. Someone will give us a lift."

Laura thought longingly of home. If there was to be no

Small Hall how wonderful to go to Mum. But where was Mum?

"We couldn't go—not without we knew Mum was there."

"Course she's there. Where else?"

"We 'aven't 'ad no letter since before Christmas," Laura reminded him.

"Then we oughter find 'er. Anyway I'm going. You can do what you like. I'm takin' Tim along of me."

Laura sat up in bed.

"Andy Clark, you know I 'ave to look after you. You 'eard our mum say so. So where you goes I go. But I wish you'd give Miss Justworthy a chance like."

Andy got out of bed.

"Well, I won't. I'm goin' 'ome. I don't want no cat food." A glorious memory came to him from the past. "What I wants is fish an' chips."

When it came to running away, it was Andy who made all the plans. Neither Laura nor Tim wanted to live with Miss Justworthy but, however little they liked the idea, they would have stayed put. They had no idea what plans Andy was making for all he would say was, "I'm gettin' thin's fixed up. I'll tell you when the time comes. For now, the less you knows the better, for what you don't know you can't talk about."

On Saturday Miss Justworthy called on the Elks to make the final arrangements.

"I do wish," said Mrs. Elk, "we could have got news of the mother before we leave. It must be all of nine weeks since the children heard."

Miss Justworthy sympathized.

"It is worrying. The inquiry of course goes through the

school, and the head has, I know, written to the proper authorities. There must, I think, be an answer soon. Probably the reason is something quite simple. So many of the parents are appalling correspondents."

"When there is an answer," Mrs. Elk begged, "will you see Laura writes to us. Here is our address. We thought it would be safer with you."

Miss Justworthy put the address away in her bag. Then she spoke in her usual rather grating, brisk way.

"I am putting the children to sleep in my spare room. The boys will share the bed and I am fixing a camp bed for Laura."

It was on the tip of Mrs. Elk's tongue to suggest that putting the boys in one bed was certain to lead to a fight but she bit it back. The children were in Miss Justworthy's care now. It was not her place to interfere.

Elk said, "I'll be across with the parcels and the food rations after the children have left for school. It's morning school this next week."

Miss Justworthy nodded.

"But come as early as possible. I am run off my feet and can't hang about. I have arranged, as you know, that the children will have their midday meal in the school canteen. Well, I think that's all. Good-by."

The Elks looked after her, their hearts feeling like lead.

Martha whispered, "If only something better could be arranged."

"But it can't," said Elk. "We must just have faith that it works out better than seems likely."

Sunday afternoon the children wrote their letters home, which of course made no mention of running away. Then Andy, first having made sure the door was closed, told Laura and Tim his plans.

"Mr. and Mrs. Elk's leavin' right after breakfast. We'll be in school so I reckon they'll drop off our thin's at that Justworthy's on their way. So after school dinner we'll go round to her house, she'll be out a 'course."

"Suppose she's in?" Laura interrupted.

Andy was confident about that.

"She won't be. She's out on her bicycle all day, everybody knows that. Then we'll take what we needs of our thin's and be off. No one won't notice. Why should they?"

"She'll notice we aren't there when she comes home," Laura pointed out.

"Let her," said Andy. "What can she do? We'll be 'ome by then. And Mum won't make us go back, not when we tell 'er about the cat's meat."

The Elks had given a lot of thought to what to give the children as parting presents. In the end they had decided on money.

"They haven't had their sixpence from home since before Christmas," Elk reminded Martha.

"Money would be nice," Martha agreed. "But I'd be afraid they'd lose it. I mean it's not likely they'll give it to Miss Justworthy to look after. And Tim can be ever so careless and so can Andy come to that."

"I tell you what I think," Elk suggested. "Let's give each of them ten shillings but not in a note, which is easy lost, but in half-crowns. Four half-crowns is not something you can throw away by mistake like a note is."

So on Sunday evening at bedtime the Elks gave their presents. They did their best to give them in a cheerful way for they did not want any tears. They were proud when they succeeded.

"Fancy, even Laura didn't cry," said Martha marveling. "I thought you gave the money ever so nice, dear."

Elk, too, was surprised.

"What's got to be got to be. Suppose even little children can see that. And the money was a surprise. Why, young Andy turned that red with pleasure it might have been twenty pounds."

It was the Elks' generous presents which kept the parting cheerful. The children had not until then had any money and it was a flaw in Andy's arrangements that there was none. It was unlikely whatever lorry they got a lift on would be going to Mansfield Road, or even to South East London, so they might need buses, and twelve half-crowns were more than would be needed. Miserable as it was to say good-by to the Elks and Small Hall, they were going home. By tomorrow they might see Mum. The children had never worried as the grownups were doing about what had happened to Rosie. Until they were evacuated she had never written to anybody. Likely enough she had just stopped doing it. The children did not like writing letters themselves so they knew how their mother felt. Even the absence of the Christmas parcel was forgotten. Maybe she'd come on Easter Monday and bring it then.

Monday's plans went like a good watch except for one thing—it poured with rain all day. This meant that Miss Justworthy did much of her day's work on the telephone instead of on her bicycle, so she was in the house when the children arrived after school dinner.

The children had been sent to school wearing the raincoats and boots the Colonel had bought for them. Miss Justworthy met them on the doorstep.

"Take off those wet things and give them to me. Never

bring wet clothes into the house. Your room is at the top of the staircase on the left. The bathroom is opposite. You had better unpack and put on your house shoes."

In the bedroom Laura and Tim faced Andy.

"Suppose she stays in all day," Laura whispered. "What shall we do?"

That was Andy's finest hour.

"She won't. I got it fixed. If it's still rainin' by two o'clock, one of the boys is goin' to telephone. It's to say Mrs. Sims, his foster mother, is took bad and gone to hospital."

"Is she?" Tim asked.

"Course not. But rain nor no rain she'll 'ave to go and while she's gone we'll be off."

Sure enough at two o'clock the telephone rang. Miss Justworthy called Laura.

"I have to go out; there is an emergency. You will find a bowl of potatoes which want peeling. Can you make a cottage pie?"

Thanks to Mrs. Elk's efforts Laura could.

"Yes. I think so, but Mrs. Elk always watched."

"Well, I've no time to watch. In the larder you will find some meat already minced, and potatoes to cook for it. Plan to have the pie hot by six o'clock."

The door had hardly shut before Andy was dashing round looking for their boots and raincoats. He quickly found them hanging on a line in the scullery.

"Come on," he said. "Thank goodness we're off. I bet that meat she said was in the larder is cat's meat."

While they had waited for the boy to telephone, the children had found shopping bags rather like the ones they had had when they arrived at Charnbury and into them had put their night things, washing things, house shoes and a set of underclothes. Laura, to be sure she had it with her, had changed out of her school gym slip into her beloved, if outgrown, blue frock. Elk had left a substantial box of food in the kitchen, which included several jars of Mrs. Elk's homemade jam.

"Seems a cruel waste leavin' all that for the likes of 'er," said Andy.

Laura pulled him away from the box.

"With our gas masks, we can't carry no more nor we got. Come along or she'll be back."

By crossing a field the children by-passed the village. This was hard going, for their boots sank in the mud. By the time they were on the main road, they were dragging along at a snail's crawl. There seemed to be unusually little traffic that day. A convoy of soldiers did go by but, of course, there was no hope of getting a lift from them.

"We might do better on one of the other roads," Laura suggested.

Tim knew that was no good.

"We'd get lost. We didn't leave one signpost showin' the way."

Presently they were coming into the next village. Andy was leading so Laura caught hold of his raincoat.

"We can't go through there. Someone will see us. They're sure to ask around when they find we're gone."

Andy stopped. He didn't like to admit it but Laura was right.

"Let's sit under the hedge and wait. Then when we hear a lorry coming we can step out."

It seemed to the children that they crouched for an hour under the dripping hedge before a lorry came. The rain poured down in straight lines like lead pencils falling out of the sky. It was extraordinarily quiet. There were no country sounds, not a baa nor a moo, not even the peep of a bird. Then at last far away they heard the sound of heavy tires splashing on the wet road. Laura took Tim's hand and the three stepped into the road.

The lorry driver was not in a good temper. He had been on the road for hours and it was skiddy. He had little to look forward to, for he reckoned he would reach London just as the siren went for the evening bombing. That would mean going straight to the shelter without his supper. Angrily he stopped his lorry when he saw the children.

"Yes, what is it?"

"Could you give us a lift to London, mister?" Andy asked.

The lorry driver thought Andy was trying to be funny.

"I've got a good mind to take a strap to you," he growled. "You might have had me in the ditch stopping me sudden like that." Then, noticing how wet and depressed the children looked clutching their soggy carrier bags, he said more gently, "Where are you from? Why don't you run 'ome and get dry?"

"We can't," said Tim. "The lady we're evacuated to doesn't want us."

"An' she'll only give us cat food," Andy added.

The lorry driver had met discontented evacuees before.

"I can't take you to London and you know it. It's not safe for you there. Run along now before there's a search party out for you."

As the lorry splashed out of sight Laura and Tim faced Andy. It had not struck the children that they might not get a lift to London. That perhaps they would have to go back to Miss Justworthy.

"She'll be back by now," said Laura. "D'you think she'll bring a search party?"

Andy dismissed the idea.

"Of course not. She doesn't want us. I guess she'll be glad we've gone."

"And havin' all that food Mr. Elk left," Tim reminded them.

There was a pause while the children tried to decide what they should do. Into that pause fell a sound. It was the whistle of a train.

"There's a station down there," said Tim.

Laura remembered.

"It was called Abasford till the name was took down to confuse the enemy."

"If there was a train going to London," said Andy, "we got the money. We could go." He crossed the road and climbed a gate. "The station must be at the bottom of this field. I can see smoke."

With no more discussion all three children climbed the gate and hurried as fast as the mud would allow down the field.

At the end of the field was a wire fence and below it a steep bank, at the bottom of which were the railway lines.

"Even if we could get over the fence," Laura said, "we couldn't get down that bank, not without falling."

Andy was scared the train they had heard would leave without them, but he could see Laura had a point. Almost certainly if they did climb the fence they would roll down the bank onto the line.

"Come on then," he agreed. "Let's follow the fence. It must end some place."

The fence ended at the beginning of a tiny platform, at

which was standing the train they had heard. As far as the children could see there was no one on the train, and it had stopped smoking so it didn't seem to be going anywhere.

Andy studied it.

"If it was to move it would go London way for the other way is Charnbury."

"If nobody isn't about," said Tim, "could we get into the train so we stopped gettin' wet?"

Andy looked at Laura.

"Couldn't be no 'arm in that, could there?"

Laura was doubtful. You were supposed to pay on trains. Still, they had the money so they could pay when somebody came for it, and it did seem stupid to get any wetter when there was a train doing nothing.

"All right," she said. "Come on. Let's get in."

The Shelter

THE CHILDREN took off their dripping raincoats and put them on the rack. The relief from getting out of the driving rain into the comparative warmth of the railway carriage made them drowsy. Soon they were asleep. They woke with a start to find the train moving.

Andy went to the window. It was dark outside and the absolute blackout did not allow a chink of light to show anywhere, but Andy had a good sense of direction.

"We are goin' backwards," he said. "I reckon the next stop will be Charnbury."

Laura got up and joined Andy at the window.

"Where'll we go from there?"

Andy was listening to the engine.

"Shouldn't wonder if it was London. The engine's the other end of the train so it's pushin' not pulling."

Tim was at the other window.

"This'll be Charnbury. I see a blue light."

Owing to the fear of enemy aircraft, no station was allowed more than tiny blue lights and the same was true of railway carriages. Though the children had not traveled by train they, of course, knew about the lighting arrangements.

"I don't see how we'll know if it's Charnbury," said Laura. "You know the name was took away."

Andy had not been allowed to help remove the name from the station but, like all the other small boys, he had watched the operation. It had never struck him then that it might be inconvenient to others as well as to Germans. Then, as the train stopped, they heard voices.

"Come on," Andy whispered. "Let's hear what they say. The platform's the other side."

The voices were those of a man and a woman.

"What you doin' here on this terrible night, missus?" the man asked.

"I brought a hot pork pie for Mr. Struthers," she explained. "George from the signal box told me the train was delayed like."

"Careless talk costs lives," the man said reprovingly.

The woman laughed.

"That's right. I always knew you was a German. But when I heard the train was waiting at Charnbury"—the children nudged each other—"I said to myself I'll take me Tom somethin' 'ot. He can do with it."

"Is it true there was a nasty road smash this afternoon?" the man asked.

"That's right. A skid on account of the rain. It was started by that Miss Justworthy who looks after the evacuees; well, her bicycle skidded and a lorry what tried to avoid her goes into the church wall."

"Any hurt?"

"Both Miss Justworthy and the lorry driver is in hospital. They say she's bad. Well, I better take Mr. Struthers his pasty. The train's not moving yet, is she?"

"No. Seemingly the soldiers what we're carrying got held up by flood water."

The woman had moved off. Her voice came from farther down the platform.

"Who's using careless talk now?"

The children sat down again.

"I wish I could get 'old of that pork pie," said Andy.

Laura thought over what had been said.

"Do you suppose," she whispered, "anyone will think to look for us if Miss Justworthy isn't there to tell them?"

"I wish I knew how long this train was stopping," said Andy. "I bet I could get to Miss Justworthy's without being seen and bring us something to eat."

Tim squeezed closer to Laura.

"I'd go better. I wouldn't make as much noise as Andy."

Laura was surprised to hear the authority in her voice. She was nearly eleven but at that moment felt grown-up.

"Neither of you are going anywhere. If it's soldiers as that man said this train is waiting for it will go fast, so we'll soon be in London where we can buy something."

Quite soon after that the soldiers arrived. There was first a roar of motor bicycles. Then came lorries and finally the sound of men carrying rifles getting into the train. The children made themselves as small as possible and crouched in the two corners farthest from the door, Laura and Tim one side, Andy the other. Every second they expected the door to be flung open and swarms of soldiers to pile in. Presently the minute blue light came on. Then, with a bit of a clank, the train started towards London.

"No one's come," Andy gasped.

"That's not saying they won't," Laura whispered. "There's

the corridor, so no one speak except in a whisper."

At that moment the door of the carriage creaked open.

"Don't say nothing," Laura whispered. "Maybe they won't see us."

With no light, it was impossible to guess who had come in, but it sounded like one person. They heard him grunt in a pleased way as if he was glad to sit down. Then they heard the sound of his kit bag being laid on the seat and a knapsack being opened. There was the rustle of paper and the champing sound of someone eating hungrily. It was more than Tim could stand. Being excited at the thought of running away he had eaten very little of his school lunch and now he was aching with hunger. He spoke in quite a loud voice.

"He's eating."

The soldier was startled.

"Who's that?" he asked. Then from a pocket he took a flashlight. He laughed at what he saw.

"Kids! Three little kids!"

Laura felt insulted.

"I'm nearly eleven and Andy is nine. Only Tim's proper little. He's six. He won't be seven till August."

The soldier put out his light. Then he came across and pulled down the blinds on their side.

"Where you goin'?"

"London," Andy answered. Then he remembered what the lorry driver had said, so he added, "We're going to see our dad. He's a sailor and he's got leave."

The soldier sat down again. Then he yawned for he was tired after the long wet day. He took another bite at his food. With his mouth full, he asked, "You kids hungry?"

"Starvin'," said Tim.

They could hear the soldier foraging in his knapsack. Then he held out a packet of chocolate. The children could see his hand and the chocolate in the blue light. To be sure it was divided fairly Laura took it.

"Thank you." She struggled to sound convincing. "We could have had sandwiches but we forgot."

The soldier scarcely heard her for he was nearly asleep. His answer was a loud snore.

Laura broke the chocolate into three pieces. It was chocolate with nuts in it, the sort that had long vanished from the Charnbury sweet shop.

"Wonder where he got it," Andy marveled as he chewed his piece.

"It was awfully kind of him to give it to us," said Laura.

Tim licked his fingers.

"I wish it was more. It's only filled a small bit of me I'm so hungry."

"Try and go to sleep like him," Laura suggested, looking towards the sleeping soldier. "When you wake up we'll be in London and we can have as much to eat as we want. No one's come for tickets so we got plenty of money."

Whether it was the chocolate or the cosiness of being out of the rain, they were soon fast asleep.

It was noise that woke them. The train had stopped, and outside were the most terrifying sounds. The roar of guns, the whine of falling bombs and the crash as they landed. The noise was not continuous but like a thunderstorm, sometimes moving farther away, sometimes back overhead.

Though the children had never been in an air raid, the descriptions of them from the more recent evacuees had taught them what to expect.

"We did oughter be in a shelter," Laura said.

Andy turned to speak to the soldier. But there was no shadowy figure in the blue light. Then the door opened and he was back.

"Look, kids, there's a blinger of a raid on in London. We're leavin' the train here and goin' to a shelter. Did you say your dad was meetin' you?"

For a second Andy nearly spoke the truth. Then the certainty that, if the soldier knew they were running away, he would see they were sent back to Charnbury stopped him.

"Yes. Dad's waitin' for us."

The soldier still hesitated.

"Well, if he's not there you tell the ticket collector and he'll show you where there's a shelter. So long and good-by and good luck."

The children heard the slamming of doors as the soldiers got out of the train and the shouts of sergeants trying to be heard above the guns. Then the tramp of feet as they marched away.

"I wish we could pull up the blind," said Andy. "That George whose granny was killed said the searchlights is smashin' when there's a raid."

Laura was firm.

"Well, we can't look. Someone will see our blind isn't down and come for us."

"I don't see how they can send us back," Andy argued, "even if they do find us. Not with that Justworthy in hospital or dead. They wouldn't let us live in her house alone."

At that moment, with a great deal of jolting, the train began to move again. It went at a snail's crawl, but it did move.

"That's good," said Tim. "Let's 'ope the next stop's London."

The train driver naturally supposed, now the soldiers had got off, that he had no passengers. So, with the willing help of his stoker, he set off as fast as he dared for the siding where his train was to spend the night.

"I got a good mind not to go 'ome but see this out in the shelter here," the stoker said. "This raid is a shocker."

The driver looked at the sky.

"I shall go home to our shelter. The missus will worry if I don't. Besides, you know how raids are. It might be better my way, I shouldn't wonder if they were trying to get the station."

The stoker looked up at the searchlights crisscrossing the night sky overhead.

"Please, Gawd, they don't hit it before we get under cover."

The children, never having been in an air raid, had no idea whether this was how all air raids were. But now they had no soldier to keep them company, Laura and Tim were scared. They did not know the difference between guns and bombs, so the roar of the British guns scared them more than the screeching whistle of the German bombs.

Even Andy felt lonely in his corner seat. He joined Tim and Laura, squeezing up against them for comfort.

"I 'ope a shelter is near. You remember that Beaty who used to write the letters for Mum. Well, in one Mum said she ran to the shelter the instant minute the siren went."

Laura, trying not to let the boys know her teeth were chattering, said with a confidence she did not feel, "Sure to be one close. One of the new exacuees told me there was one in most streets."

The train was now off the main line, though the children did not know it, and edging into a siding. Suddenly it stopped and at once the little blue light in the carriage went out.

Against the noise of the air raid the children did not hear the slamming doors nor the shouted "good nights and good luck" of the driver, stoker, and guard. They only knew that once the train noise had stopped the noise outside was worse. Andy pulled up the blind in the nearest window.

"No 'arm in lookin' out now the light's gone out." Then, after a pause: "The platform ain't this side, must be the other." Andy went across to the door and into the corridor. "There ain't no platform 'ere neither." He came back to the others. "I think this is one of them places where they puts trains out of the way till they're wanted."

Laura, rigid with fright, managed to say, "What shall we do then? Is it safe to stay here?"

"Course not," said Andy. "You 'old onto me and, Tim, you 'old onto Laura. We're goin' to find a shelter."

Air raids, for those with time and the inclination to look, could be strangely beautiful. The searchlights raking the skies for the bombers were like huge slim icebergs pointing to the heavens. The guns, as they fired, filled the sky with their belching lights, and fires started by bombs lit the whole scene in a red glow.

"Cor!" said Andy, "that beats any fireworks!"

"Oh, do go on, Andy," Laura implored. "We'll be killed, I know we will."

Tim, now he was out in the air, was more conscious of his empty stomach.

"I'm hungry," he shouted above the noise, "and you said, Laura, I could 'ave as much to eat as I wanted when we got to London."

At that moment a man's voice spoke.

"Who's there?" And the children found themselves picked out by the beam of a light. Then the voice said in amazement, "Kids! What are you three doing here?"

The children told the same story about their father being on leave, but the man was interested in nothing but getting them under cover.

"Come along. All this can be sorted out later. I'll just hand you over to the shelter marshal."

On the way to the shelter the man explained that he was part of a team of fire watchers, all of whom were trained to put out incendiary bombs. It was on the tip of Andy's tongue to tell the man that the warden at Charnbury had trained people too, but he bit it back in time. Instead he asked the man if he'd ever had to put out a bomb.

The man, holding Laura by one hand and Tim by the other, had little time to talk.

"Lots," he said. "Come on, the shelter is just at the end on the right."

They stopped and turned into what seemed an underground tunnel. They went down perhaps twenty steps, then pushed through two layers of sacking. The outside one was slimy with grime and rainwater. They found themselves in a low-ceilinged basement. It was dimly lit, but the children could see it was full of bunk beds. They were in neat rows with a passage to walk down between them. In a corner was a door marked LAVATORY. At a table a man wearing a tin hat was seated.

The man who had found the children pushed them forward.

"I'm on duty fire-fighting at the station where I found these. It seems they were expecting to be met by their father who's on leave from the navy."

The shelter marshal looked worried.

"I'm afraid I'm full but I'll manage. If you see the father send him here. If not I'll hand them over to the police in the morning. How's the raid?"

Up to that moment the children had thought everybody in the bunks was asleep. But the moment the man asked about the raid dozens of heads were raised.

"It's a shocker. We've got the lot tonight. Must have got it in for us."

A woman called out, "It's for me, dear. Must have 'eard it was me birthday. They're celebrating."

There was a lot of laughter and during it the fire watcher disappeared. Underground in the shelter the noise of the raid was so muffled it was quite difficult to hear it.

The shelter marshal looked at Laura.

"Where do you three come from?"

Laura did not answer for she did not dare say Charnbury and she could not think of anywhere else. Luckily Tim, by now ravenous, spoke his mind.

"I'm starvin'. If I don't eat somethin' soon I reckon I'll die."

The shelter marshal laughed.

"You look as if you could do with a wash but you don't look like dyin'. We 'aven't much down 'ere but the canteen should be 'ere any minute."

A woman dressed in a one-piece suit, trousers and top all in one, scrambled out of her bunk.

"Give them 'ere, Marshal. I'll see they're all right. Between us we'll squeeze 'em in. You won't 'ave long to wait," she told Tim. "Our canteen ladies will be along any minute." She handed each of the children a biscuit. "Meanwhile these'll 'ave to do."

The woman, whose name was Mrs. Smith, had several friends. Among them they doubled up to give the boys a bunk. Laura was squeezed in with Mrs. Smith.

"Maybe you better take your frock off," Mrs. Smith said, "or it won't 'alf be crushed by the morning."

Laura took off her beloved blue frock.

"It was ever so pretty. I wanted our mum to see it, but I was give it when we was evacuated so even let down it's short and a bit tight now."

Mrs. Smith was going to ask about their mother but at that moment the clink of mugs was heard. Into the shelter came three women dressed in green wearing tin hats. Two were carrying wooden containers, each of which had twelve mugs. The third had a tray piled high with a variety of buns.

"You got any money?" Mrs. Smith asked.

But already Andy and Tim, half-crowns at the ready, were joining the people clustering round the food. Laura was going to hold back because she had taken her frock off but Mrs. Smith gave her a push.

"You run along before your brothers scoff the lot. Those ladies in green, W.V.S. they're called, has seen a lot worse than your petticoat."

The children had a glorious meal, starting off with mugs of a hot drink rather like a soup and going on to buns. Tim ate five.

Back in bed Laura found that Mrs. Smith had been thinking about them, perhaps even talking about them to her friends.

"That was a whopper about your dad meeting you, wasn't it? I mean no one would fix it for you three to come to a station of a nighttime. Not with a raid every night."

There was something about Mrs. Smith which made

Laura trust her. She didn't seem the sort of person who would send them back to a Miss Justworthy who didn't want them. On the other hand, one look at her and you knew she wouldn't let children out of her sight until she was sure they were all right.

"It wasn't a real big whopper," she said. "Dad *is* in the navy and he's comin' on leave." Well, that was sort of true, all sailors did have leave. "But he and Mum don't know we're comin'. It's a surprise like."

"They'll get more'n a surprise when they see the police with you. For that's who'll take you 'ome. Nobody wouldn't let three kids like you wander on your own around London. Why, you might fall into a bomb crater and nobody wouldn't know. If I 'adn't to go to work I'd take you 'ome meself. Oh well, we better get some sleep. Don't you pay no attention when I slip out in the morning. I 'ave to go as soon as we 'ave the All Clear—it's the only time I get to clean me place."

This news soothed Laura. If Mrs. Smith could slip out on the All Clear they ought to be able to manage it too. She would find the boys as soon as Mrs. Smith left and then they would go home to Mum. On this glorious thought she fell asleep.

Mansfield Road

LAURA WOKE out of a deep sleep wondering where on earth she was. Far away she could just hear the friendly wail of the All Clear. Then it came back to her. The woman pulling on slacks and a shirt was Mrs. Smith, who last night had shared her bunk with her, and in the next row of bunks Andy and Tim were sleeping. She would have liked to thank Mrs. Smith but she didn't dare. Nice as she was she would likely enough interfere and see someone went with them instead of letting them go on their own. Then that someone would find out Dad wasn't on leave and that might mean their being sent back to Charnbury.

Laura was quite right about Mrs. Smith. She was not certain she believed Laura's story. It was so unlikely three children would be sent alone to London at a time when an all-night air raid was almost a certainty. So as she left the shelter she accosted the shelter marshal.

"I'd let them kids what came last night sleep on. They was ever so tired, and scared too, shouldn't wonder."

"O.K.," the marshal agreed. "As soon as I see a copper

I'll tell him about them. They'll know what did ought to be done.

As soon as those who left on the All Clear had gone, Laura slipped out of the bunk and went to the one where the boys were sleeping. With some difficulty she woke Andy.

"What is it?" he asked crossly and in far too loud a voice.

"You got to get up and so's Tim," Laura whispered. "If we stays here they'll put a copper on to look after us."

That was enough for Andy. He was out of the bunk in a flash and, with a hand over his mouth to keep him quiet, was waking Tim.

The shelter marshal had tidying up to do before he could leave the shelter, so he was busy sweeping the steps when the children crept out from behind their bunks.

"Let's wait," Laura whispered. "He's sure to have other cleaning to do."

The shelter marshal had. As soon as he moved away from the entrance, the children slipped through the two layers of sacking, climbed the steps, and were in the street.

It was still not quite light and a sort of fog hung in dirty gray wisps to the buildings.

"First thing," said Andy, "is to get some breakfast."

Tim looked around.

"Where? Nothin's open yet."

"Anyway," Laura pointed out, "we can't waste time if we're to catch Mum before she goes to work."

The children were not London born for nothing. They could find their way round even in the very bombed-out London where they found themselves. So it was not long before they had placed themselves on top of a bus headed for S.E.8, though it took two changes before they were in walking distance of Mansfield Road. As they traveled, the children were chilled into silence by what they saw. It was true they had been away a year and a half and had become used to the country, even accepting it as beautiful. But at the back of their heads had always been the knowledge that Charnbury was temporary, that behind it lay London, which was home. Now, gazing out of the bus windows the children, already tired from lack of sleep, felt a sort of hollowness inside them. Of course London was dirty, you expected that, but they hadn't expected everything else: All the spaces where houses had been. The acres of tarpaulin covering broken roofs. The muslin in place of glass in hundreds of windows. The half houses with bits of their insides exposed. The terrifying spaces where streets and houses had once been. The sinister-looking barrage balloons cluttering the skies to keep the German planes from flying low. The number of arrows pointing the way to shelters. There was also a change in the people. Always before, Londoners, even in the hungry years of unemployment, had been gay people, always glad of a joke at which to laugh. Now they were still gay but it was not a general gayness. It was full of private jokes, which only real Londoners who had stayed in London throughout the bombing, understood.

"Lucky they finished early last night," one woman said. "I need a bath. It's two weeks since I got time before work."

"That'll be nice, dear," another replied. "We was wondering where the smell came from."

"We can't get no water down our street," an old man told the bus.

"Surely got a standpipe?" someone asked.

"I can't wash under a standpipe," the old man protested. "What would the neighbors say?"

"Did you hear about the warden?" somebody asked. "He 'ad an unexploded bomb dropped down the gratin' in the gutter."

"Did 'e go after it?" a voice called.

"Of course not. 'E gets one of them bomb-disposal chaps. Well, the chap comes and he fixes to be lowered on a rope, but if 'e finds the bomb's goin' off he'll give a sharp tug and he's to be brought up pronto."

"So I should 'ope," someone interrupted.

"Well, down 'e goes," the storyteller went on, "and a minute later there's a almighty tug on the rope. So those who aren't on the rope falls on their faces and the rest 'auls the chap up. 'Is it goin' off?' they asks 'im. The bomb-disposal man was quite green with fright. 'Oh, the *bomb*,' 'e says, 'I don't know about that, but what I do know is no one can't go after it. There's a rat the size of a dragon down there.' "

The passengers, all but the children, rolled about with laughter. The children had not really followed the story. They knew rats. Why should the bomb-disposal man, whoever he was, mind one? Why did people fall on their faces?

Suddenly they were in their own High Street. It seemed wonderfully unchanged. The church where they had gone to Sunday school had lost part of its spire. The fish and chip shop had vanished and a shelter had taken its place, but on the whole, leaving out broken roofs, the street looked marvelously the same as it used to.

Andy got up and the other two followed him.

"Funny," someone said as they vanished. "You don't often see kids these days. Wonder what they're doin'?"

Downstairs the woman conductor stopped the bus.

"Where you goin'?" she asked in a friendly way.

" 'Ome," said Andy. "Our dad's a sailor an' he's come on

leave."

"Oh lovely! Have a nice time."

Tim liked the girl so he added, "It's not far now. We live in Mansfield Road."

The children were off the bus and the girl had rung to tell the driver he could restart it. So no one saw her clasp her hand to her mouth nor the worry in her eyes as she watched the children hurry down the High Street.

It was not more than ten minutes' walk to Mansfield Road. Now that the children were almost in touch with home they stopped feeling tired and began first to walk fast and then to run.

"I can't wait for Mum to see us," Tim gasped.

"Only one more turning," Laura panted.

Tim as usual thought of his stomach.

"I 'ope she 'as somethin' for breakfast."

They were round the corner. There was Mansfield Road, S.E.8 stuck up on the wall. But where was Mansfield Road? Where all the condemned houses had been there was nothing. Nothing at all. It was impossible to see where number 4 had once stood. There was just a large open space covered in rubble.

Laura heard a strange singing in her ears. Then the ground began to spin round. She fell down unconscious. Tim started to scream, one piercing scream after the other. Andy felt an anger so violent he had to do something about it. From the rubble he picked up some large stones and hurled them at where number 4 might once have been.

Within seconds of the start of Tim's hungry hysterical screams people arrived. The first was one of the local wardens.

"What's all this, sonny?" he called out. Then he quickened his speed to a run as he saw Laura lying on the ground.

Andy stopped throwing stones.

"We come 'ome. We lived at number 4."

At both the warden's post and at the Town Hall there was a file about the family in number 4. The warden tried to remember what it was all about. Then a name floated into his mind.

"Name of Clark?" he asked. He was kneeling beside Laura. She was coming round. "What we need is a cup of strong tea with plenty of sugar."

Unnoticed, a small, bent old lady had joined the group.

"All right, warden," she said. "Bring the children in to me. I've got the kettle on."

The warden looked at her gratefully.

"That would be kind, Mrs. Oswald. Then I'll go back to the post and find Mrs. Gregson."

The warden picked Laura up in his arms and led the way to what had been the last house in Mansfield Road. It had somehow missed the blast and was more or less in one piece. It was the only house left standing.

Mrs. Oswald walked beside Andy. She peered at him short-sightedly.

"You won't remember me, I don't suppose, but I remember you. Just a baby you was when you went away."

"Where's our mum?" Andy asked.

Mrs. Oswald seemed to think about that. For there was quite a pause before she answered.

"I reckon the warden knows. None of us wasn't here when the bomb fell. A land mine it was. Most of the 'ouses 'adn't a brick left; yours was one. The Town 'All re'oused everybody but I wouldn't go. What I say is, if a bomb's got your

name on it, it's got your name on it. No good in runnin'
away."

Down the track across the rubble where Mansfield Road
had been came a little fat woman dressed as a warden. She
had been on duty all night so her blue uniform was gray
with dust. The other warden looked glad to see her. He
paused so she could catch them up.

"Oh, Mrs. Gregson! These are the Clark children from
number 4."

"We're taking them to my place, Mrs. Gregson," Mrs. Oswald explained. "The little girl fainted. I got the kettle on."

Mrs. Gregson evidently considered herself in charge. She
nodded acceptance of Mrs. Oswald's offer. Then she said,
"If she's one of the Clark children, her name is Laura."

"How do you know that?" Andy asked. "We ain't never
seen you before."

Mrs. Gregson might be short and fat and dusty but she
exuded dignity.

"I was Mansfield Road's warden. So it was my job to
know all my people and where they was of a nighttime. I
got you three down as being in a place called Charnbury."

They had reached Mrs. Oswald's house. It had been at-
tached to another, but somehow the other house had blown
away without taking Mrs. Oswald's house with it. Some
pieces were gone. She had only half her front doorstep left,
but she kept what remained as clean as if it was a whole
step. She had no glass in any window, just muslin. Instead
of a roof she had a piece of tarpaulin. But inside everything
was as neat and cosy as she could make it. In one corner of
the room was Mrs. Oswald's bed.

"Put the little girl there, Warden," she said. "I expect you
could all do with a cuppa and I've just enough cups. The

W.V.S. lady gave me six when she saw most of what I 'ad
was broken."

"I'm hungry," said Tim.

Mrs. Oswald looked worried.

"I haven't got much, dear. Well, there isn't much in the
shops, is there, but I expect I can manage some bread and a
scrape of jam."

The warden was anxious to get back to his post. It was
time he was home but this case must be reported to the
Town Hall.

"I'm going to the post," he suggested. "If I took the boys
there the day wardens will get them something to eat."

Laura had been lying quietly apparently taking no interest
in the conversation. But now that the ground had stopped
turning round she felt better and could hear what people
said. She sat up.

"Andy and Tim aren't goin' nowhere not without me.
Mum said I was to look after them."

In the end the children, fortified by cups of strong tea
with a lot of sugar in it, were fetched in a Civil Defense car
and taken by Mrs. Gregson to what she called a Rest Center.

"A Rest Center is where we puts people who is bombed
out; it's where they can live until we gets them moved to
somewhere."

The Rest Center had been some kind of church, but no
one would have known it if they hadn't been told. The
ground floor had tables all down the middle. At one end
was a huge stove with easy chairs round it. In the chairs
were sitting rather battered-looking men and women. A few
children were dashing around getting under everyone's feet.

Mrs. Gregson pointed to the stove.

"There's one thin' you can be sure of in a Rest Center and

that's a bit of warmth. Most of those brought in here suffer
from shock and so must be kept warm."

There were several women helping in the Rest Center.
Mrs. Gregson introduced the children to a Mrs. Hallow, who
was dressed in W.V.S. green, but first she drew her to one
side and whispered to her.

"I wish," Laura murmured to Andy and Tim, "we could
see Mum."

"Well, she must 'ave moved," Andy pointed out. "She
couldn't stay, not with our 'ouse blow'd away."

Mrs. Hallow came smiling to the children.

"I hear you haven't had breakfast."

"No," said Tim, "and we're starvin'."

"Well," said Mrs. Hallow, "come and sit down and I'll
see what I can get. The night cooks have gone off duty and
the day cooks aren't here yet. But I'm sure we can find something."

The "something" started with bowls of porridge and went
on to scrambled eggs—rather peculiar eggs the children
thought, used to country eggs, not eggs out of a packet. The
breakfast finished with a large plate of toast spread with
margarine. There was tea to drink.

While the children were eating, Mrs. Hallow got on to
someone important at the Town Hall. She explained who
she was and where she was.

"I have the Clark children here from number 4 Mansfield
Road. I mean that's where they did live."

It was a man at the other end.

"I heard they've turned up. They should be at Charnbury in Dorset. The telephone line is very bad after last
night's raid but as soon as it's repaired I'm getting on to
them to say the children are safe, and I hope we can send

them back again."

"I learn from Mrs. Gregson nobody knows what's happened to the mother."

"Too right," the man agreed. "She was last seen running to the shelter just as that bomb fell on Kinton Street."

Mrs. Hallow said, "I thought you'd got all those people accounted for."

"We've accounted for all those who were killed as far as we know, but there was no Mrs. Clark nor anything found to suggest she had been there. We can't be quite sure, for passing cars picked up some of the wounded and took them to hospitals."

Mrs. Hallow said, "Well, I suppose the hospitals know who they've got?"

"They think they do," the man agreed, "but there's still a few queries. It is possible some car driver who picked up a casualty got the name wrong."

"What do the children know?" Mrs. Hallow asked.

"Nothing. They were to have been told a little, for we wanted them questioned about any friends of the parents. But then the old Colonel on whom they were billeted died and it was necessary to move the children to a new billet. They were to have been told directly they settled down."

"Is there a father?" Mrs. Hallow asked.

"Yes. But he's a sailor and the Admiralty office reports he is at the present time unobtainable."

"Is there anything I can do?"

"Yes, try and make friends with the kids and get the names of any friends of the mother. If we had that they might know what happened to her."

The children were finishing their breakfast when Mrs. Hallow rejoined them. She sat at the head of the table with the boys on her left and Laura on her right.

"Is it true that you three have come all alone from Dorset?" She managed to sound admiring. "How did you do it?"

Andy was, of course, the main spokesman. After all, running away had been his idea, but he was perpetually interrupted by Tim and occasionally by Laura. Mrs. Hallow heard the whole story about the Colonel and the Elks, and how happy the children had been except for the indignity of going to bed at six o'clock and the Colonel being so fussy about eating.

"Still, 'e was ever so nice really," said Laura. "We was all sorry 'e died."

"Special sorry," Tim added, "cause we was to go to Miss Justworthy."

Miss Justworthy, recovering from concussion in hospital, would have had a relapse if she could have heard the children describing her. She, poor thing, directly she had recovered consciousness had remembered them and got a nurse to telephone the warden at Charnbury to make arrangements for someone to move into her house to look after them. She had been told not to worry, all was being seen to, for she was too ill to be told the children were missing.

Andy described to Mrs. Hallow with great drama the railway journey and their arrival in London.

"So then we was took to this shelter," Andy explained. "Then first thing we took buses to come 'ome."

Mrs. Hallow knew Laura had fainted once and didn't want her doing it again. So she said calmly, "It must have been a horrible shock. I suppose you had a lot of friends in Mansfield Road."

The children looked at each other.

"There's that Mrs. Oswald that give us tea this mornin'," said Tim. "She knew us before we was 'vacuated."

Andy was indignant.

"But she didn't really for I was seven. Nobody couldn't call seven a baby."

Laura tried to explain.

"You know how it used to be. We know'd everybody sort of. But the 'ouses were condemned so people was always movin' away."

"Our dad was often unemployed so he knew lots down at the Labor Exchange," Andy added.

"Did your mother work?" Mrs. Hallow suggested. "I mean after you were evacuated?"

The children nodded.

Andy said, "You know how all the soldiers comin' back from that Dunkirk left all their guns and tanks and that behind. Well, our mum makes them."

"I expect she has lots of friends at the factory," Mrs. Hallow suggested.

Suddenly all three children remembered.

"Beaty!" they said.

"Beaty wrote us regular on account she writes better than Mum," Laura explained.

"And at Christmas she sent us a card," Tim reminded Laura. "It said, sorry your mum can't come for Christmas she will be ever so disappointed."

"Oh, dear God!" Mrs. Hallow prayed silently. "Let that card have been posted after the Kinton Street bomb." Out loud she asked, "Did you get that card in time for Christmas?"

The children looked at each other. When had Beaty's card arrived? Then Tim remembered.

"Course we did. Two days before, Mrs Elk said she was glad someone had let 'er know so she needn't make up the bed."

Beaty

MRS. GREGSON took the children to her house to give them baths and to change their underclothes.

"Can't help gettin' mucky on a train," she explained cheerfully. "These wartime trains is chronic. I suppose no one 'as the time to clean 'em."

Mrs. Gregson lived in a little flat. She had, she said, been lucky so far, as her building was undamaged. It even had its original roof. Her instructions were to keep the children happy and interested as long as she could.

Meanwhile the most urgent inquiries were being made to locate Beaty. The authorities at the Town Hall had been very worried since before Christmas about what had happened to Mrs. Clark. It was right and natural that the public wanted to help when they saw casualties scattered about a street, but what they could not learn to do was to report back to somebody explaining exactly what they had done. The result was that it was possible for some well-meaning person to rush a patient to a hospital without any real information about them, so patients had sometimes been admitted under the wrong name.

Nor were casualties necessarily taken to the nearest hospital. During a raid it was a common sight for stretchers to be waiting in queues to get into casualty departments, so it was natural for the public to think the patient they had picked up would get a better chance at some hospital farther away. Was it possible the missing Mrs. Clark was in some hospital under the wrong name? It did sound as if Beaty, if she could be found, knew what had happened. Otherwise why would she have sent the message on the Christmas card?

Mrs. Gregson, while she washed the children, told them about her work.

"It must have been a coupla' years before the war started that I 'eard about becoming a warden. The things we learned! Laugh! You see, never 'avin' seen no bombing we didn't know what it really was like."

Andy thought he would like to be a warden.

"Our warden back in Charnbury, he learned people how to put out incendiary bombs. Can you do that?"

Mrs. Gregson dismissed incendiary bombs with a gesture.

"Course I can. But before the war, like I was telling you, we used dummies like they have in shops to show clothes. We laid them around and then put them on stretchers in the ambulances. Makes one laugh to think of it now, all so clean and tidy, not a bit like the real thing."

After the washing and cleaning up, Mrs. Gregson took the children back to the Rest Center. There Mrs. Hallow met them.

"You must go and get some sleep," she told Mrs. Gregson. "I know you had a terribly busy night." To the children she said, "They'll soon be serving dinner. We have dinner at noontime now. It's some kind of stew; it smells delicious.

Come down to the basement and I'll show you where you'll sleep tonight."

The basement was a regular shelter with tiers of bunk beds just like the ones they had slept in the night before.

"I expect you could do with a sleep after dinner," Mrs. Hallow suggested. "From the sound of things you didn't have much sleep last night."

The children were tired but, much more, they were anxious. Why did nobody take them to see their mother?

"Our mum must be livin' somewhere," Andy said. "Why don't we see 'er? Then we could go to the shelter along of 'er tonight."

Laura looked pleadingly at Mrs. Hallow.

"Everybody is ever so kind but it's Mum we want."

Mrs. Hallow looked at the children. In spite of being tired and drawn Laura was, she thought, a charmingly pretty child. Andy trying so hard to be the man of the party, Tim so determined he could do anything Andy could do. She was getting fond of the children. She decided on a half-truth.

"At this very minute the wardens are trying to find Beaty. They think she has your mother's address. It may take a little time because there are several munition factories in this district and we don't know her surname. You are sure you never heard it?"

The children were still carrying their paper carrying bags. They were rather empty now because Mrs. Gregson had kept their underclothes to wash. Laura fumbled in the bottom of hers and brought out a crumpled collection of letters. They were all there, starting with the first one, which began: "Dear kids, Your dad is a sailor now . . ." to the Christmas card: "Sorry your mum can't come for Christmas. She will be ever so disappointed. Beaty."

Mrs. Hallow looked at the letters and card.

"Do you mind if I read these?"

Andy said, "You must be a real lady. Sir said no real lady nor gentleman would read other people's letters."

"He was quite right. But if I have your permission I might find something in them which will help."

While the children explored the shelter Mrs. Hallow read the letters. When the children rejoined her she said cheerfully, "Beaty sounds a grand girl. I'm sure she'll know where your mother is. I hope your dad gets some leave soon. In almost every letter your mum says how much she is missing him."

"I 'ope they lets us stop in London," said Andy. "Charnbury was all right when Sir and Mr. and Mrs. Elk was there. But that Justworthy we was supposed to go to she's a shocker she is. Feeds her 'vacuees cat food."

"An' makes 'em do all the work," Andy added.

To make sure Mrs. Hallow understood it was not just they who didn't like Miss Justworthy Laura added, "Nobody doesn't like her."

"Well," said Mrs. Hallow, "the Town Hall have managed to get in touch with the local Civil Defense. It seems you can't go back today anyway as the lady you were to have stayed with is in hospital, but I should make up your minds that you won't be left in London. I should think you'll be reevacuated."

"Let's see what our mum says," said Laura.

While the children were having their dinner Mrs. Hallow again rang the someone important at the Town Hall.

"About the Clark children. I have seen the letters and card written by this Beaty. What we are looking for is a well-educated girl. She has written to the children at the mother's dictation I should say. Could you ask around the factories for an extra-bright girl, perhaps a scholarship type?"

The someone important sounded pleased.

"I believe we may have found her. If it's the right one she was planning to be a teacher. She had a place at a teacher training college. The factory wanted her to work in the office, but she refused, saying she had come to make munitions. They are having the dinner break now but someone will see her as soon as she is back. They don't know her Christian name, but her initial is B. Her surname is Mac-Donald."

Twenty minutes later Beaty MacDonald, walking back to her machine, was stopped by the foreman.

"Come into the office a minute. There's a warden here wants a word with you."

"The sooner this is settled the better," the warden explained to Beaty. "This case shouldn't have dragged on like it has, but no hospital reported a case having been admitted without a name."

Beaty was a nice-looking girl with dark curls showing under the cap all the women had to wear in case their hair caught on the machines. Now she smiled.

"Well, I can explain that. I was on my way to the shelter when that bomb fell in Kinton Street. I suppose I got a bit of the blast for right away I couldn't remember where I was. Then I remembered seeing Rosie ahead of me. She was running because the siren had gone. I ran up to where the bomb had fallen. A man from a car asked if I was looking for anyone. I said, 'Yes, it was Rosie,' or maybe I said, 'Rose.' Anyway we found her. She wasn't dead but terribly injured about the head. I suppose I looked a bit rough and the guns were starting up so the man said, 'You go to the shelter I'll see to Mrs. Rose. I'll take her to St. Hilda's. It's very good there for head injuries.' "

The warden was taking notes.

"So you went into the shelter and the man put Mrs. Clark in his car?"

"That's right," Beaty agreed. "I must have passed out later 'cause I woke up in hospital. They said I had shock."

"I don't wonder," said the warden. "Did you ever visit Mrs. Clark?"

"Of course. Luckily I found her bed, for they'd got her down as Mrs. Rose."

"Didn't you explain her real name was Clark?"

Beaty looked ashamed.

"I should have. I sent the kids a card, for she was going to them for Christmas, but I didn't tell them she was in hospital, for she wouldn't want them upset at Christmas and then it was too late. I mean they knew her as Mrs. Rose and there didn't seem any reason for me to tell them differently. You see, she could talk by then and could tell them herself if she wanted to."

"Have you seen her lately?"

"Every weekend. She's fine. Sits up in a chair now."

"The three children are in London. Do you think she'd like to see them?"

Beaty's eyes shone.

"In London! Well, I never! I'll say she'd like to see them!"

The warden closed his book.

"We will, of course, have to hear what they say at St. Hilda's. Anyway we'll keep in touch with you to let you know what happens."

After a good dinner of stew followed by apple pie the

children went down to their bunks to have a sleep. They were awakened by the Civil Defense man in charge of the Rest Center.

"There's been a telephone message about you three. The W.V.S. lady, Mrs. Hallow, is fetching you in a car in about ten minutes."

Andy looked stubborn.

"What for? Where we goin'? I'm not going back to that Justworthy I tell you straight."

The Civil Defense man had no use for rude, disobedient small boys.

"You'll go where you're told. But as it happens where you're going with Mrs. Hallow is to St. Hilda's Hospital. You're to see your ma."

Air Raid

ON THE WAY to St. Hilda's Hospital Mrs. Hallow tried
to prepare the children to expect their mother to look different.

"Your mother has been very ill," she explained.

"Must've been," Andy agreed. "She's been in 'ospital two
and a half months. That man told us at the Rest Center."

"Did he tell you about her injuries?"

Andy did not like the man in charge of the Rest Center.

"No. Proper close mouth 'e is. Rather bite your 'ead off
than talk civil."

"I'm sure he didn't mean to be unhelpful," said Mrs. Hallow. "I think he's rushed off his feet. But what I was going
to tell you was that your mother's injuries were to her head.
They've had to shave all her hair off."

The children tried to picture their mother with no hair.
No one had curls in their family but Rosie had tried to look
as though she had them. She couldn't afford a permanent
wave no matter how she saved, but with back-combing and
pins she got a frizzy look.

"In one of Mum's letters what Beaty wrote," said Laura, "she said Mum was savin' for a permanent for Dad's leave."

"Mostly when people's 'eads is shaved it's on account of nits in their 'air," said Tim.

Mrs. Hallow resisted a shudder.

"It's nothing like that. She has had an operation to remove some broken bone. Her head was shaved for that. You won't be able to pay her a very long visit for the sister in charge of her ward says she is still weak. But she's getting on well and expected to make a complete recovery."

"We did ought to bring her flars," said Laura. "People always do when they go to see someone what's in 'ospital."

At that stage of the war flowers were frowned upon by the government. If you had space to grow anything you were expected to grow vegetables. Andy knew Laura knew this. He apologized for her.

"She knows you can't have flars no more. She helped dig up Sir's big flar border."

"Your mother won't expect flowers," Mrs. Hallow comforted Laura. "You don't expect flowers in February."

"In Charnbury there was," said Tim. "There was snowdrops and crocuses. I growed them in my garden."

Rosie was in a large, long ward. Her bed was in a corner so she could look out of the window. When Mrs. Hallow led the children into the ward she had no eyes for the window; she was watching the door. In fact all the patients who were well enough to look were watching the door. So, indeed, was any nurse with a second to spare, for Rosie, with her changed name and her children who had run away from Dorset to visit her, was considered a romantic figure. "It's like something out of a book," they told each other.

Rosie, though she was thinner, had changed hardly at all.

She had a bandage round her head but the nurse had fastened onto it a paper rose left over from Christmas, so she looked quite smart. The other women in the ward had clubbed together so that the children could have a little party. At that time almost all food was rationed, but from some hidden store a few chocolate biscuits had been dug out and there was a small dish of sweets. For Laura there was also a piece of ribbon for her hair and for the boys a handkerchief each, made out of an old blouse.

Rosie held out her hands to the children while tears poured down her cheeks.

"You don't 'ave any right to be here, and your dad'll take a strap to you when he knows, but, oh my Gawd, am I glad to see you!"

Presently, when the first emotion had died down and the children were eating the treats provided, Andy asked about his father.

"When's Dad gettin' leave, Mum? 'E said 'e might come sudden like to Charnbury but 'e never."

"I wish I knew," said Rosie. "I was tellin' the doctor I reckon a sight of 'im and I'd walk out cured."

Laura broke in.

"Those new 'vacuees what come to Charnbury after the bombing, one of them had a grandmother what was killed. And 'e said 'is father was brought 'ome. Compassionate," she stumbled over the word, "leave it was called."

"Well, I'm not dead," Rosie pointed out.

"But you nearly was," said Tim.

That was when Rosie produced her trump card. One which even during a war earned awe and respect.

"I was more'n three weeks on the danger list."

The children gasped.

"An' nobody didn't know?" asked Tim.

Rosie smiled.

"Oh yes, they did. Beaty did. 'Mrs. Rose is on the danger list,' they said. 'You can visit whenever you like.' An' she did. I didn't know nobody else, not then."

"Well, I think they did oughter 'ave given our dad 'passionate leave," said Andy.

Rosie beckoned the children to come nearer.

"You mustn't say this 'cause as you know careless talk costs lives, but I think they can't get to 'im. Once he said in a letter, just before he sailed that was, 'Next time you see me I might be wearin' a fur coat.' "

The children looked puzzled, trying to imagine their father in a fur coat.

"What did 'e mean?" Laura asked.

Rosie drew them even closer. They could only just hear what she said.

"I asked Beaty. I knowed she wouldn't talk. And she said she reckoned he was far north. Norway or someplace like that."

Mrs. Hallow came back.

"Sister thinks I ought to take the children home or you'll be tired, and anyway I want them in before the siren goes. If they are still here I'll bring them back tomorrow."

Rosie looked anxious.

"Don't let them stay here one day more than they need. I want 'em sent back where they come from."

Andy almost shouted.

"We're not goin' there—not ever! Do you know, Mum, that Miss Justworthy feeds her 'vacuees cat's meat?"

"An' makes them do all the work," Tim added.

"I don't care what she gives you," said Rosie. "You aren't

stoppin' in London an' that's flat. Your dad an' me talked it all over and we agreed, no matter 'ow 'ard it was, that you was to stay in the country."

"But Dad doesn't know Sir is dead."

Rosie, from the table beside her, produced Mrs. Elk's letter.

"This was in my bag." She read out, dropping an aitch here and there: "I am grieved to inform you that the Colonel is dead. He was taken very sudden at a Home Guard parade. Changes will have to be made but not before Christmas so please do come as arranged." She folded the letter and put it back on her bedside table. "The day this come I had Beaty copy it and sent it straight off to Dad. So I reckon 'e knows."

"If 'e can get a letter why can't 'e get 'passionate leave?'" Andy demanded.

Mrs. Hallow could explain that.

"My husband is in the navy. Letters can get through. I expect they use airplanes to drop them or submarines to deliver them, but that does not mean they can get a man home."

It was time to leave. It was obvious that tears were not far away. Laura clung to her mother.

"Oh Mum! Can't we stay somewhere we can see you every day?" Her voice broke. "I don't want to leave you in 'ospital."

Tears were again beginning to trickle down Rosie's cheeks.

"I wish it could 'appen. But it can't. It's the war, dear."

Mrs. Hallow took one of Laura's hands and gently pulled her from her mother.

"I tell you what," she promised, "if it's humanly possible, wherever you are sent tomorrow, I'll manage to bring you in to give your mother a good-by kiss."

Back at the Rest Center the inmates were having an early supper to fit in before the raid started. The children were told to sit at the end of the table. Andy was put next to a boy of about Laura's age who said his name was Alf.

"You bombed out?" Alf asked. "*I* was two months back."

From the new evacuees at Charnbury Andy had learned that bombed out meant your home was destroyed. He was not letting Alf get away with anything.

"We was bombed out too but we wasn't there. We was 'vacuated. But our mum was hurt bad. She was ever so long on the danger list."

"I was 'vacuated once," Alf said, "but I didn't stay more'n a week. I don't like the country and you should 'ave 'eard the old girl I was billeted on. Do this! Do that! She wanted me to sit with 'er to eat, but I never. I sat on the doorstep same as I do 'ere."

"Where you goin' now then if you're bombed out?"

"My mum's got a sister over at Shoreditch. She's makin' room for us. Mum saw 'er today."

Andy was interested. So some children did stay in London. "You don't mind the air raids then?"

Alf's tone expressed his scorn of air raids.

"Na. Course I don't." He lowered his voice. "Matter of fact it's a bit of all right if you know 'ow. Look."

Under the table he pulled up the sleeve of his jersey and showed Andy four watches.

"Cor!" said Andy filled with envy, for he had never owned a watch.

The boy pulled down his jersey sleeve.

"It's easy if you know how. Last night when our place went I 'eard the jeweler's on the corner 'ad gone. So I nip out of the shelter quick and there was these watches all amongst the glass and that. I'd a got more but there was light from a place that was burning."

"What 'appens if you're caught?"

"Send you away I reckon. Lootin' they calls it. They're all down on that."

Laura had not been able to hear what Alf was telling Andy, for he spoke in a whisper. But she could see Andy was interested and she had a feeling Alf was not a good friend for him.

"I wouldn't 'alf like a watch," Andy said with envy.

Alf at once became a businessman. Picking up looted stuff was something he was clever at, but getting rid of what he had found was more difficult. Few people approved of looters and some might go to the police.

"Got any money?"

Andy nodded. He had spent most of one half-crown on buns and a hot drink in the station shelter and on bus fares, but he still had three left.

"A bit," he said cautiously. "Say five bob."

Alf looked round and saw Laura was watching him.

"Wait till later. Five bob ain't enough. I might take seven-and-six but not 'ere. Your sister's lookin'."

After supper everybody collected their belongings and waited for the siren.

"They're late tonight," somebody grumbled. "I don't like 'em being late, it generally means they're up to something."

All Londoners at that time knew their local barrage balloons. These floated at all times over their heads like great silver ships. If the enemy were attempting anything special the number of barrage balloons might be doubled for these kept the enemy planes from flying low.

Now someone said, "If the barrage balloons is anything

to go by it's a very special night. There's hundreds up."

At that moment the sirens began to wail, followed almost at once by the sound of gunfire. Everybody went down the stairs to the basement. On the stairs Alf pulled at Andy's sleeve.

"Here's the watch. You got the money?"

Andy was terribly torn. Of course he wanted the watch. Wouldn't anyone who had never owned one? But it was wrong and he knew it.

"I've not made up me mind."

Alf was smart. He knew how difficult it would be once you had felt a watch on your wrist to hand it back. He pushed a watch into Andy's hands.

"Wear it for tonight. If you decide you wants it, seven-and-six in the mornin'. If you gives it back, no 'arm done. O.K.?"

Andy waited to try the watch on until he was in his bunk. It was, he thought, a beautiful watch, perhaps made of solid silver. It had a good black strap and it could be all his for just three half-crowns. And it wasn't stealing. That had been done already, if it was stealing to pick up something in the road.

Andy was so busy admiring his watch that he did not hear the crash of the guns outside, nor the howl of the bombs. It was, as somebody had warned, a special night, for an attempt was being made to bring a convoy of ships up the river. Nor did Andy hear Laura climb out of her bunk and onto his. She was shivering. The first he knew was when she said, "Oh Andy, can I stay along of you? I'm scared."

Andy had taken off his jersey and shorts, so the watch was exposed. The basement was deep, so a few lights were still on. Hurriedly he put his arm with the watch on it under the blanket.

Scared of what? I reckon this is what 'appens every night."

"No, it's extra bad. I 'eard someone say. Suppose we was hit?"

Andy listened to the sounds outside. It certainly was noisy.

"Not down 'ere we wouldn't be."

At that moment there was the howl of a falling bomb followed by the crash of smashing masonry. Then, even nearer, the sound of a second bomb. That second crash shook the whole Rest Center. No one in the basement heard the third bomb but they heard the floor above them fall in and felt dust and rubble cascade onto them like rain. At the same moment all the lights went out.

Trapped

LIVING IN the country and not being allowed out after dark the children had not been given flashlights. For most people in cities, however,—children and grownups alike— a small, low-powered torch run on a battery was as much a part of their outfits as their gas-mask boxes. So, almost directly after the bomb had exploded, tiny twinkling lights appeared all over the shelter.

The shelter part of the Rest Center was run by a shelter marshal. He was especially picked for the job, for so many of those who slept under the Rest Center had already been bombed out. It was accepted by those in authority that a strong man was needed in case there was any hysteria.

The shelter marshal here was an ex-regimental sergeant-major with a voice to match his title. Now, having given himself a good shake to get rid of dust and rubble and felt around to see if there was much damage, he took a deep breath and roared, "Quiet everybody. Now is anybody 'urt?"

Nothing could have been more comforting to those in the shelter than the sound of that huge voice. It was clear from the very way the marshal spoke that the danger of being trapped alive under fallen masonry did not exist. That did not mean there were not whines and grumbles. What was "hurt?" It needn't be a great injury. There were smaller sufferings that should receive sympathy. So at once a chorus arose, all the sufferers speaking at once.

"My back got another jar just where the bricks got it last night."

"I think somethin' 'it me 'ead, for I never knew nothink after that last crash."

"One of my legs seems queer. I think somethin's fallen on it."

The shelter marshal allowed this wail for a minute or two, then he took another deep breath.

"Now don't nobody move. I'll be round to see each of you but what I want now is blood. Any of you bleedin'?"

This silenced all the complainers for no one could offer actual blood. He turned on a powerful torch.

"Right. Now, as far as I can see, all passages is fairly clear. I got all your names and addresses and I'm now coming round to check on each of you."

Laura clutched Andy's arm. She was going to say "Get Tim" but her fingers had fastened on the watch. Having no torch she could not see what she was holding but she could feel.

"Andy! It's a watch! Whose is it?"

With that sergeant-major around, Andy was longing to get rid of the watch.

"It's nothin'," he said unstrapping it. "Somebody lent it me. I'll put it under the pillow."

"It belongs to that Alf, doesn't it?" Laura demanded. "I knew 'e was up to no good."

Andy was cross and scared. He wished he knew where Alf was so that he could give him back his watch. It wasn't his fault he had it. He had said from the beginning he didn't want it.

The shelter marshal's strong torch was coming down the row in which were the children's bunks. By its light Tim from his bunk saw the outline of Laura's head. He scrambled out of his bunk and skipped over to her. He started to tell her he had wondered where she was but the shelter marshal roared first.

"Did I or did I not say nobody move? Who moved then?"

Tim's voice sounded like the squeak of a scared mouse. "Me!"

"And who's 'me?' "

Laura had to help. Had she not promised to look after the boys?

"It's Tim Clark. He's my brother."

The marshal's voice softened.

"I know. You're Laura, Andy, and Tim Clark. I'll be along with you in a minute."

Laura carefully felt round Andy's pillow. As far as she could feel the watch was completely hidden. She dare not mention it to Andy, for sharp-eared Tim was bound to hear. Instead she moved up the bunk and sat on the pillow.

The shelter marshal, when he reached Andy's bunk, turned his strong light on the children.

"Glad to see you three are all right. If I was you, as soon as you feel like it, I'd get back to your bunks and go to sleep."

Tim said, "We was told the ladies would come round with buns and that."

The shelter marshal moved on his way.

"They may not come tonight, but if they don't I've got something you can have. Lovely hard candies sent special from America."

Tim was sleepy so Laura tucked him into her bunk to have him within touching distance.

"If he brings sweets round I'll see you get yours," she promised. "Then you can have it when you wake up."

Soon the shelter marshal was able to report that no one was seriously hurt, so now he would try and communicate with what he described as "them up above."

By the time he had started this, which seemed to mean a lot of banging and shouting, Tim was asleep so Laura was able to hear the story of the watch. This Andy told her in a far less truculent tone than he would have used before the bomb exploded. For somewhere he had a muddled memory of hearing about punishments coming to evildoers.

"I never thought to keep it," he whispered to Laura. "I was only wearing it just for tonight. You want to look at it? It ain't 'alf smashin'."

Laura didn't want to look at the watch. It was stolen property to be got rid of as quickly as possible.

"If he comes back with them sweets we could ask where Alf sleeps. What's his other name?"

"I don't know. 'E never said. But I got to find 'im. Maybe someone would lend me a torch so I could look."

Laura was so shocked she raised her voice.

"Andy Clark! You heard what the marshal said. Nobody's not to move. If he says we can move then we'll all go and look for that Alf together. If not you keeps his watch till we gets out."

Andy was not pleased. He was certain if he could borrow a torch he'd find Alf in no time. But it was no good arguing with Laura. If he tried to get out of the bunk she'd know, and Laura, quiet as she was as a rule, was quite capable of making a row if it was to look after him or Tim.

Either the raid was no longer overhead or the effect of the exploding bomb had dulled all other sound. There was certainly less noise from up above. In fact, the only loud noise was the knocking of the shelter marshal trying to contact the rescue workers. In fact, there was so little noise that first Andy and then Laura, still sitting on the pillow, dropped asleep.

It was lucky the children did sleep, for it saved them a lot of the fuss and anxiety from which those who were awake suffered. One of the troubles of being trapped by bomb damage was the way rumors spread. None of the trapped knew anything about air-raid damage except what they had picked up, so they swallowed any whisper that got around. The first rumor was that the air was giving out. It was nonsense; naturally, fresh air was not flowing in as it had before the bomb fell, but there was still enough to keep everybody going, especially if they lay quietly in their bunks. But the thought of suffocating is terrifying, and the moment the word suffocation got around there was panic. Of course the shelter marshal was ready for it.

"What's all this?" he roared, a noise through which somehow the children slept. "Who says they have heart palpitations? Our air's O.K. Maybe not as fresh as it was but it will last many an hour yet. Which, by my calculations, we shouldn't need. I reckon they'll 'ave us out of 'ere in a coup'la shakes of a rabbit's tail."

The next scare was that the roof was coming in. For there was a sudden crash and clatter. Again the shelter marshal was ready.

" 'Ow do you think the heavy rescue is going to get you out if they don't clear the stairs? I was just going to tell you I could hear them working when that noise come."

It was about three in the morning when the children awoke. By then things were bad in the shelter. However hard the shelter marshal denied it, there was no doubt the air was getting very poor and it was increasingly difficult for him to keep the people's spirits up.

Although he could hear the rescuers working above he had made no real contact with them. An occasional faint tap in answer to his bangs on the wall was all he was able to get.

It was about then that something made the marshal think of the children and his promise of a sweet. Sweets, especially gift sweets from America, were sure to be made of the best sugar and what could be better for everybody? He found his tin of sweets and, shaking it like a castanet, marched amongst the bunks. The noise woke Tim. He sat up and shook Andy.

"Sweet time. That marshal's bringing the sweets."

"Now listen everybody," the marshal roared. "One sweet per person. And I don't want nobody giving their sweets to a child. This is medicine to be sucked slowly. Pure sugar. Nothin' to touch it."

Before the marshal reached the children the great event of the night happened. There was a rumble, and a mass of debris came cascading down where the shelter stairs had been. In the middle of the dust and rubble something was plunging about. The shelter marshal turned his torch to see what was happening when suddenly out of the rubble climbed a warden still wearing his tin hat.

To other people the warden might have looked just a very dirty man; to the people in the shelter he was St. George, the slayer of dragons. They might be short of breath but somehow everybody, even the weakest, cheered.

The arrival of the warden did not mean the people in the shelter were freed. There was a lot more digging to do first. But the warden's falling down the steps cheered everybody up, for it was obvious that if one person could get in other people could get out.

Awake, and with a real live warden added to their party, Laura and Andy began to worry about the watch again. The warden had brought another huge torch with him, so now, with the two torches flickering about, it was quite impossible for anyone to move without being seen. Actually Tim did move, for the shelter marshal passed quite close and Tim scrambled out of his bunk to speak to him.

"You promised when I woke up you had a sweet for me come straight from America, an' we never got ours 'cause the warden fell in."

"You come along of me," said the shelter marshal. "I'm not one to go back on a promise."

He took Tim's hand and led him to a shelf on which was standing the sweet tin. He took the lid off and told Tim to take three sweets.

"Suck 'em slowly and they'll do you a power of good."

Directly Tim was out of hearing, Laura whispered to Andy, "What are you going to do with the watch?"

"Give it back to that boy, of course. I should think now they're nearly through to us, people will start to walk about so I can find 'im."

Laura looked round.

"Not except for necessity they aren't walking."

Andy leaned out of his bunk and stared round. Presently he straightened up.

"Tell you what. I'll crawl. No one won't notice me under

the bunks."

"But you don't know where Alf is."

"Don't you worry. I'll find 'im," said Andy. "Now you keep young Tim busy and give me that watch."

When Tim came back Andy was gone. Laura took Andy's sweet and put it under his pillow to await his return. To keep him amused she talked to Tim about the day's plans.

"If that Miss Justworthy 'urt her 'ead I wouldn't think she'd be ready to 'ave us yet."

"I don't want to go back to 'er never," said Tim. "I want to stay somewhere we can see our mum every day."

Laura stared round the shelter but except for the light from the big torches it was far too dark to see Andy, even if he had been walking instead of crawling.

But she had forgotten the sharp eyes of the shelter marshal. The first she knew of trouble was a shout.

"What's this? What d'you think you're a-doing of?"

Then, to Laura's horror, she saw by the marshal's strong light Andy gripped in his arms. She wasted no time.

"Come on, Tim, take hold of me hand. Our Andy's in a bit of trouble, I got to see he's all right."

By the time Laura and Tim reached Andy and the shelter marshal, the warden had joined them and had found the wrist watch which Andy was holding in his teeth. It was the warden's duty to know all that went on in his area, and he was well aware that watches had been stolen from a bombed-out jeweler's. Also, he had a shrewd idea who the thieves were and he did not think Andy was one of them.

"Where'd you get this watch?" he asked.

Andy, breathless with fright, could only whisper.

"It isn't mine. I was lended it."

"That for a tale," said the warden. "I'll hand you over to

the police when you get out of 'ere. There's several more missin' they'd like news of."

By now everybody in the surrounding bunks was interested and murmurs of, " 'Tisn't right stealing from the bombed-out." "Children's a menace at a time like this."

Andy was not the crying sort but he was getting near it.

"I tell you I didn't take no watch, I couldn't 'ave, we wasn't 'ere."

At that moment Laura, holding firmly on to Tim's hand, came to Andy's defense.

"That watch don't belong to my brother," she said. " 'E was lent it just for the night. 'E's to give it back first thing."

The shelter marshal was, in spite of his loud voice, a kind man. He didn't like to see a child blamed without proof.

"Perhaps," he suggested to Andy, "you could find whoever lent you the watch."

It never crossed Laura's mind that some would think she was telling tales. All she cared about was Andy.

"Course 'e can. 'Is name is Alf. 'E's bombed out and is staying in the Rest Center same as us."

What might have happened next nobody knew, but suddenly an enormous woman with red hair appeared apparently from nowhere. She leaned down and shoved her face into Laura's.

"An' what Alf might you be talkin' of? It's true me and my boy Alf spent yesterday in the Rest Center. An' why not? Bein' bombed out, it's our right, isn't it? But that don't give no one the right to say Alf stole a watch 'cos he never. As innocent as the day 'e was born my Alfie is and no one won't tell you different."

The warden could stand no more. He knew Alf's mum by sight and was sure he was on the track of the missing watches.

"Well, where is Alf?" he asked. "Let's see what he's got to say."

Alf, cowering under his blankets in his bunk, was quickly found. Gripped by the warden all the braggart went out of him.

"What d'you know about this watch?" the warden asked.

"You don't know nothin', do you, dear?" his mother said, but the warden had felt Alf's arm. He rolled back the sleeve and exposed the other three watches.

The warden pocketed these and the one he had taken off Andy.

"I'll give these to the police first thing. Lucky for you you're under age or you'd get shot like enough. That's what they do with looters."

Alf's mum evidently felt enough fuss had been made.

"We're leavin' as soon as we get out of 'ere, goin' to me sister's down Shoreditch way."

"Poor old Shoreditch!" murmured the warden. "Had trouble enough I'd say without bein' landed with young Alf."

The shelter marshal shepherded the children back to their bunks.

"Come on. You've time for a bit of shut-eye. I shouldn't wonder if you go to sleep now, the next you'll know you'll be eatin' breakfast."

Mrs. Seecom

THE SHELTER MARSHAL was nearly right. With the help of ropes and a fire-brigade ladder, all the trapped were able to climb out of the shelter. It was then about six in the morning and there was nothing left in the Rest Center on which to cook or eat breakfast. But a little thing like that did not put off the experienced local people. In no time they had sorted out those people who had somewhere to go and those who had nowhere, and were leading the "nowhere" queue towards the food. To Laura's great relief Alf and his mum were not in the breakfast queue.

"Nor I wouldn't be if I was them," Laura thought. "Alf's mum won't want Alf told off by the coppers."

The place where breakfast was waiting was the basement of the Town Hall. Everybody in London seemed to eat the same breakfast in wartime. Once more there was porridge followed by the same peculiar scrambled eggs and finished off with as much toast and margarine as they could eat. But this time there was no going to Mrs. Gregson's house for a bath. Instead, with the clean clothes she had washed the day before in a parcel, Mrs. Gregson came to the Town Hall and washed the children in a large washroom there.

"Now," she said when they were reasonably clean and tidy, "you got to come and see one of the 'high-ups.' You wouldn't believe the trouble it causes when one of you 'vacuees runs away."

The children were taken to a corridor and sat on a bench where they waited to be called. Mrs. Gregson stood farther up the corridor watching them as if at any moment they might make a dash to escape.

Andy was very good at talking with his mouth hidden by a hand; he did this now.

"Remember, you two," he said, "no matter what the high-up says we're not going to that Justworthy and we're not splittin' up. What we wants is somewhere to stay at nights just till Mum's O.K. again."

Laura leaned forward so her hair hid her mouth.

"We're going to see Mum. Mrs. Hallow almost promised. Mum won't let us go except it's all right."

Andy put his hand back over his mouth.

"Lying in bed there she don't know. How would she know we was living on cat's meat?"

Tim never bothered who heard what he had to say.

"What I'd like just till Mum's O.K. and Dad's 'ome is we could stay along of the Elks."

That was so stupid both Laura and Andy turned on him.

Laura said, "You know that's what they wanted but there isn't no room in Mr. Elk's mum's cottage."

Andy added, "And they can't move into the cottage what Sir left them on account of the land girls."

Tim looked round the corridor where they were sitting. It looked very dreary.

"Seems there aren't no place for us. No place at all."

Andy felt, as the present head of the family, he ought to be able to say something cheerful but he couldn't find anything. Tim was right. There was no place for children in a war. No place at all.

Presently the warden led the children and Mrs. Gregson down several passages to a small room with the name *Colonel Ponsonby* painted on the door. Inside there was a man in a grand version of Civil Defense uniform sitting at a desk. Beside him, to the children's joy, was Mrs. Hallow. They all beamed at her.

"We didn't know where you were," said Andy.

"Had you heard our Rest Center was hit?" Tim asked.

Mrs. Hallow held out a hand to Laura.

"This is Colonel Ponsonby, children. He's very important in Civil Defense."

Colonel Ponsonby turned to Mrs. Gregson.

"You were on duty all night I hear, so you should be in bed. You have done a splendid job looking after these three, but we can now take them off your hands. The mother, as you know, is in St. Hilda's. We'll forward you the children's address when we have it."

Mrs. Gregson said good-by to the children.

"Andy, do make up your mind not to run away again. You've no idea the trouble you caused, and with a war on we just haven't the time."

When Mrs. Gregson had gone, the colonel told the children to sit down.

"Sorry, it'll have to be the floor. Chairs are scarce. Now, let's hear about you. You left London with all the other children back in '39, I suppose."

Andy treated the colonel with the same respect with

which he had treated Colonel Stranger Stranger.

"That's right, sir. They tried to separate us but it was all right. Sir took all three of us."

The colonel looked at the notes in front of him.

"I understand he died just before Christmas. What was your host's name, by the way?"

The children looked at each other.

"We always called him Sir," said Laura.

Tim remembered shopping expeditions.

"In the village he was called Squire."

The colonel stiffened like a dog who scents a rabbit.

"Was this place you were billeted called Charnbury?"

"That's right," said Andy.

"Then your Sir was called Colonel Launcelot Stranger Stranger."

Dimly the children knew they had heard that name before. Laura nodded.

"He was never called that. Mrs. Elk always called him just the Colonel."

The colonel stiffened again.

"Mrs. Elk! You don't mean Elk was still with him?" He turned to Mrs. Hallow. "Elk had been Colonel Stranger Stranger's batman for years. Best batman in the army." He turned back to the children. "What's happened to the Elks now?"

The children all helped tell the story.

"Sir didn't give his house to Mr. Elk," Laura explained, "because it was too big."

"Instead he gave him his cottage," Andy broke in. "But that's let for the duration to Mr. Gedge for his land girls. He's got four of them and they're all whoppers."

The colonel stopped Andy there.

"Half a minute. If the land girls weren't in the cottage would the Elks have taken you to live there?"

The children nodded. Then Laura said, "Mrs. Elk cried when she told us we couldn't go with them."

"Then what's happened to Small Hall, the house in which you were billeted?" the Colonel asked.

"Babies," said Andy. "Lots came to Charnbury expectin' babies so it's to be a sort of hospital."

The colonel looked at Mrs. Hallow.

"Might be something worth looking into there." He did not explain to the children what he was talking about but evidently Mrs. Hallow understood.

"It's a long shot but it's worth looking into."

The colonel studied the papers in front of him.

"Miss Justworthy on whom you are billeted . . ."

Andy looked fierce.

"I'm not going there, she feeds her 'vacuees cat food."

The colonel suddenly sounded like last night's shelter marshal.

"You'll go where you are told without fuss. Why? Because the person who has agreed to the arrangements is your mother."

That cut the ground from under Andy's feet. If Mum had joined the enemies what chance had they?

"I don't believe Mum said we could go," he said, but in a subdued voice. "I just don't believe it."

"We thought you might think that," Mrs. Hallow agreed, "so I am taking you to see her."

Laura said in a small voice, "I think Miss Justworthy's in 'ospital so we couldn't go today."

Mrs. Hallow nodded.

"Yes, poor woman. But we understand she is allowing you

to stay there and someone is coming in to look after you."

The children said nothing. What was there to say? Andy felt all the courage had been kicked out of him. He had felt so grown up planning their escape and so much had turned out so well, but now he was back being just one evacuee, someone who until he was billeted was only a nuisance.

Laura saw Andy was giving in and in a way she was glad. Even being near Mum she didn't want to spend another night in London. Besides, it might be all right if the somebody who came to look after them was kind.

Tim had accepted that in Miss Justworthy's house cat food was eaten, and his stomach rebelled. But, like the other two, he could feel he was powerless. Everybody—all the grownups including, apparently, Mum—were banded against them. They would be prisoners in Charnbury until the war was over, and that might go on forever.

Mrs. Hallow drove the children to St. Hilda's. They did not stay long, for Rosie was tired and inclined to be tearful. But she made it perfectly clear that it was her wish they go back to Charnbury.

"I don't know what your dad would say if he knew what you'd been up to. Making trouble when everybody's been so good. And imagine you being bombed last night! Lucky you were rescued before I 'eard or I think it would 'ave finished me." She hugged the children. "Write regular, won't you, and I'll get Beaty to write for me. Now you're in charge, Laura. See the boys be'aves nice and . . ."

What was to come after the "and" no one knew for Rosie cried too much to be heard.

The children were sent by car to Charnbury. With them traveled two old people who had been bombed out the night before. The driver was a Mrs. White—a W.V.S. driver. She was quite nice, but the children wished she was Mrs. Hallow

It rained all the way and the drive seemed interminable. There was a bright spot when they stopped for lunch at a W.V.S. office and had a splendid meal of hot sausage rolls and cake. It was there the two old bombed-out people left them.

They seemed sad to have arrived; the old lady cried and the old man said, "We don't want to give no trouble but we didn't want to come away. We've always been Londoners and we don't reckon my wife's sister wants us."

Laura, climbing back into the car, felt like crying herself. So many people like her and the boys being sent to places they did not want to go to with all their belongings in paper carrier bags.

Tim, feeling something the same, suddenly burst out, "I wish Sir hadn't gone and died."

Charnbury was a well-run village and somehow had managed to do all that the government had demanded of it. They had taken in their share of evacuees. The farmers grew what they were ordered to grow. On the whole they stuck by the law; if occasionally a piglet was fattened where ministry officials would not find it, when it was killed there was a fair share-out to all those in the know. The ambition of all in Charnbury, and villages like it, was to play their part in the war effort without too much interference from officialdom. This they had succeeded in doing until now, when the disappearance of the Clark children had stirred up a hornet's nest.

"How was we to know Miss Justworthy was goin' to meet with an accident?" the warden grumbled to the policeman.

"The way they carry on in London!" said the policeman.

"When was the children last seen? Who by? As if we'd the time to see every kid 'ome from school."

It was however an order from county level that really upset all in charge at Charnbury.

"London says County A.R.P. [Air Raid Precautions] reported on the telephone the children will be coming by road this afternoon."

"But where to?" Mr. Silt muttered. "We haven't a corner to put them in."

"The voice on the telephone said, leaving no room for argument, London suggests arrangements are made for a caretaker to move into Miss Justworthy's house. Then she can keep it in good order and look after the Clark children."

Put like that it sounded so easy but where was Charnbury to find a caretaker? Everyone's house was full to overflowing. No woman could be spared even for a night.

However A.R.P. at county level could offer help.

"There is a Mrs. Seecom. She was evacuated with her child. She is a good cook and housekeeper but has been difficult to billet. She has a large family who like to visit her at weekends. This is not popular. But she would do splendidly for you as it is only for a short time. Just one thing though: get the houseowner's keys and only unlock such rooms as she wants used. With Mrs. Seecom spare space is fatal. I will send her and the child, Dulcie, right away."

Poor Miss Justworthy, racked with a headache, feebly handed over her keys.

"The spare room with an extra camp bed is ready for the Clarks. I don't want my room used, but I suppose Mrs. Seecom and the child must go there. Lock the lounge and the dining room. There is nothing else."

So when the W.V.S. car drove up to Rose Cottage, which

was what Miss Justworthy's house was called, Mrs. Seecom and Dulcie were already in possession. So much so that Mrs. Seecom was already treating the little house as her own. She was a roundabout little woman, rather like an old-fashioned loaf, the sort that was made in two halves. She wasn't kind to her figure, for she was wearing a very old green-velvet dress which had large patches on it where the pile had rubbed away.

"Come in. I've tea ready. I can't usually offer tea but I thought today's special so let's be generous."

Mrs. White hesitated. She wanted to get back to London. But all the same it was her job to see the children safely settled in.

Tea was laid in the little kitchen. A splendid tea coming almost entirely, as the children recognized, out of the Elks' box. Andy, to his amazement, found himself siding with Miss Justworthy.

"You didn't ought to have touched none of this. It was given to Miss Justworthy by Mrs. Elk to help out while we lived here."

Mrs. Seecom was one of those people who only hear what they want to hear.

"Very kind, I'm sure. Now sit down all and eat hearty."

Laura felt a lump in her throat as she looked at the jam, cake, and biscuits all made by Mrs. Elk. Somehow, though she would have disliked Miss Justworthy's handling them, it would have been right. The box was given to her. But this woman, bossing everybody in their billet, was too much. She put her chin in the air.

"I think," she said, "we should wash before we eat. Sir and Mrs. Elk both said that."

Mrs. Seecom was not accepting what she called "sauce."

"Your room . . ." she began to say, but Laura interrupted her.

". . . is the spare room at the top of the stairs. We know, thank you."

In the spare room with the door shut Laura said, "I know you don't want to wash but I had to pretend we did. That awful woman carrying on as if it's her house."

"Almost I'd rather eat cat's meat with Miss Justworthy," said Andy.

Miserably the children gazed at each other. Then Laura said, choking back a sob, "Charnbury has always been so nice, I never knew what it would be like without Mr. and Mrs. Elk."

The Other Seecoms

D U L C I E did not seem to be a trouble to anyone but, though she did not know it, she had from the beginning been one of the reasons why every householder on whom she and her mother were billeted refused to keep them.

From birth Dulcie had been enormously photogenic. As soon as she could toddle, she was sent to a stage school. She was far too young to appear professionally, so instead she danced for charities. She had already made quite a name in her neighborhood as "Little Dulcie."

After much discussion among Dulcie's loving family, it was decided when war was about to be declared that the home must be broken up and Dulcie's mum be evacuated with her—not only to look after her but to see she kept up her dancing practice.

It was the dancing practice the hostesses objected to. Cottages in Dorset, already full to overflowing, had no room for one child to tap dance, or what was described as "kick her legs about." They wanted children who helped with the farm work or in the house, then got down to homework or quiet games. Perhaps, if Mrs. Seecom and Dulcie had not moved so often, someone would have discovered the undoubtedly talented Dulcie and sent her round with concert parties which entertained the armed forces.

The children's first view of Dulcie was when they came down from their bedroom and found her wolfing into a pot of Mrs. Elk's special crabapple jelly.

"I say, go slow on that," said Andy. "Mrs. Elk meant it to last."

Laura felt Mrs. Seecom swelling with indignation so she tried to distract her attention.

"Mr. Elk left his address, and we did ought to write. We said we would. Have you got it, Mrs. Seecom?"

Mrs. Seecom scowled.

"No. Miss Justworthy may have put it somewhere safe but she's the locking-up sort. So I can't get in anywhere."

Billeting people in other people's houses had proved in many cases a difficult business. Children alone, unless hopelessly unhousetrained, could usually be coped with, but children with grownups were only rarely a success. The children did not, of course, know it but Mrs. Seecom and Dulcie were well known to at least a dozen billeting officers. The worst of it was that each new billet started off all right. Mrs. Seecom was a good cook and willing to help in the house. Naturally Dulcie soon became a thorn in the flesh. But it was the relations who really got the hostesses down. Two grandmothers, two grandfathers, Mr. Seecom, all his sisters and brothers, and all of Mrs. Seecom's somehow found vans and petrol and felt a night or two away from the bombing would do them good.

The trouble was they were so hard to get rid of.

"You won't mind my old mum sharing my bed for a

coupla' nights, will you, dear?" Mrs. Seecom would say "Dad doesn't mind where he sleeps. He'll doss down on the floor. It's the quiet they enjoy after the bombing. Well, it's our duty to give what help we can, isn't it?"

If it had only been Mum and Dad just once. But all those relations! In the end it was more than flesh and blood could stand, so at last each harassed housewife, often escorted by an angry husband, turned up at the billeting officer's desk to say, "I can't keep that Mrs. Seecom and her Dulcie a day longer."

At just such a moment, the news circulated that a woman with a child was wanted for a few weeks to run an injured billeting officer's house and to look after three children. The news had scarcely had time to sink in before telephone lines were buzzing and Mrs. Seecom and Dulcie were on a train for Charnbury.

To Mrs. Seecom one of the charms of being billeted in a house empty except for three children was the thought of spare beds, or at least of spare floors. All her family were getting cross at only being able to come down for the day. Surely, with the bombing as bad as it was, she could manage to put them somewhere for a couple of nights. On the way to Rose Cottage she had thought that she could. She had pictured jolly family weekends with plenty of food and drink, for all her relations were clever in the black market. (The black market meant cheating the rest of the country by sneaking more than your share of what was rationed.)

It had been a real shock when the temporary billeting officer had shown Mrs. Seecom Rose Cottage, with only the two bedrooms, the kitchen, and the bathroom unlocked. "The meanness of some people," she had thought.

"If you could loan me a stamp," said Laura, "I'll write to

the Cottage Hospital now and ask Miss Justworthy to send the Elks' address."

Mrs. Seecom was a good cook and housekeeper, but that did not mean she intended to wait on three strange children.

"First we must get the work done. Dulcie can't help. She has her dancing practice. If we all stay in the kitchen could you manage to practice in the passage, pet?"

Dulcie, though spoilt, was an obliging child.

"I couldn't do spins, pirouettes, or my kicks," she said, "but I can hold onto the stairs for my bar work."

"That's my girlie," said Mrs. Seecom. "Now, Laura, you can help me wash up and you two boys can wash this floor. I suppose a lot of people have been in and out. This floor looks as if a herd of elephants had marched through here."

As there was no other accompaniment Dulcie sang to keep time. So Laura dried and put away the tea things and the boys tried to wash the floor to "and a-one and a-two, knees bend, and turn."

The children were dead tired after two bad nights and all their traveling. In any case neither Andy nor Tim had ever washed a floor before. Mrs. Elk would not have considered it children's work, and at home the floor had never been washed. So when Mrs. Seecom, having wrung out the washing-up cloth and hung it to dry, turned to find the kitchen floor awash with water, Tim soaking wet, slimy with soap, and Andy equally wet as he pushed around the scrubbing brush, it was perhaps natural that she should lose her temper.

"Really! Where were you children brought up? Haven't you ever washed a floor before?"

Already Andy disliked Mrs. Seecom. Now he hated her.

"No. And I don't believe Dulcie can wash one either."

There was a faint pause.

Then Mrs. Seecom said, "That's different. Dulcie is a very gifted child and must be treated differently." She turned to Laura. "Can you mop this up?"

Mrs. Elk had taught Laura a lot but not how to wash a kitchen floor. In any case Laura was so tired she could hardly keep her eyes open. She shook her head.

"No, Mrs. Elk never told me to do that." She was so tired that she forgot to care what Mrs. Seecom thought of her. She pulled Tim to his feet and beckoned with her head to Andy. "Come on. Let's go to bed."

Mrs. Seecom, competently tidying the kitchen, thought about Laura.

"Looks as though butter wouldn't melt in her mouth but she'll need watching, that one, or my name isn't Clara Seecom."

To the children's amazement they were welcomed as heroes at school. It was morning school that week. Almost every child has said at some time, "I'll run away," but very few ever do. Now here were three who had done it. They had gone to London and been buried alive in a bombed building and found their lost mother safe and sound in a hospital.

The head teacher was a sensible woman. Of course it was wrong of the children to have run away but she could understand anyone running away from Miss Justworthy. She knew all the school would sooner or later hear of the Clark children's adventures so she decided it should be sooner.

After the roll call she said, "Laura, Andy, and Tim Clark, come on the platform."

Gingerly the Clarks stepped forward. No one ever was beaten at school, but then no one had ever run away before.

"I need not tell you children you did a very wrong thing.

You caused busy people a lot of work and worry at a time when your country is fighting for her life. We all believe that someday we shall win the war, we all pray that someday we shall know peace again, but that can only come if we all, with every minute of our time, work for it. We cannot afford to waste a second, and causing busy people to search for three missing children is wasting hours rather than seconds. Do you understand that?"

She looked at Laura. Laura had not thought of their escape to London like that, but now tears of shame ran down her cheeks.

"Yes," she whispered. "I'm sorry. Truly I am."

The teacher turned to Andy.

"And you, Andy?"

Andy was not sure. Much of the escape had been glorious.

"Well, we did find our mum."

The teacher smiled.

"We are coming to that in a minute." She looked at Tim. "Do you see that running away was naughty, Tim?"

Tim was not sure what he thought. But he knew if he had the chance to go and see Mum he'd always go.

"We see'd Mum," he said, warmed by the memory. "She got her head cut but it's nearly well now. When it is we got to find somewhere to live. Our house was bombed."

Laura was still crying, so the teacher looked at Andy.

"Now, Andy, tell us everything that happened. I gather it was you who planned it all."

Andy took a deep breath.

"It was when we found Mr. and Mrs. Elk was going to move and we were to shift in with Miss Justworthy, who feeds her . . ."

The teacher had heard about the cat's meat and was not

having the story repeated

"Start where you left the house. Which way did you go? Apparently nobody saw you."

Andy was in his element. He had never had it so good. The whole room just hanging on his words. Once or twice Tim tried to join in but a sharp "Shut up, you" quickly silenced him. Laura was delighted to leave the storytelling to Andy—and even to listen. As told by Andy, it all sounded so much less frightening and so much more exciting than it had really been. The only thing Andy left out was the bit about the watches.

When Andy reached the point when he got into the car to drive back to Charnbury the teacher stopped him. Already she had heard stories about Mrs. Seecom and there in the classroom, looking somehow exotic among the evacuees and village children, was Dulcie. The teacher could imagine how Andy might describe the arrival at Rose Cottage.

"Thank you, Andy. What adventures! But exciting as it all was, as I said at the beginning, it was very wrong. Now we will all sing 'Jerusalem' with special emphasis on the words, 'I will not cease from mental fight, Nor shall my sword sleep in my hand, Till we have built Jerusalem, In England's green and pleasant land!' "

None of the children had any idea what William Blake's poem was all about, but it sounded fine. After it they marched off to their classes, determined from that minute to help to win the war.

Miss Justworthy had put the Elks' address in her desk, which was locked in her lounge. She could not think of anybody with time to go to Rose Cottage and get the address for Laura, so she decided she must trust Laura with her lounge key. She's a good little thing as a rule, she thought, even though she did run away. I'll have to trust her. When a part-time woman from the Billeting Office came to see her she explained the situation.

"Laura Clark—you know, the family that ran away. She wants the Elks' address. Would you ask the school to tell her to come and see me on Sunday? Visiting hours are from three to four."

Life was going on its uneasy way in Rose Cottage when Laura got this message. The children did not like Mrs. Seecom because she made too free with what had belonged to Mrs. Elk. They disliked, too, the way they were expected to help in the house and Dulcie was not. On the other hand they rather liked Dulcie, who, the moment her mother's back was turned, tried to teach them the rudiments of acrobatic dancing. All three children were wild to turn cartwheels like Dulcie. It was Friday when Laura got her message and after school dinner—Dulcie had her midday meal at Rose Cottage—she told the boys about it.

"When I been to the 'ospital I shall write to Mrs. Elk as well as Mum. Lucky we got some money left for we'll 'ave to go to the shop for paper and envelopes and buy two stamps."

"I think one letter from all of us will do for Mum," Andy suggested. "It was only Sir who said we all have to write."

Before Laura's eyes swam a picture of the old man in his study with the three sheets of his very grand notepaper waiting for them. She turned to Andy.

"Andy Clark, you did ought to be ashamed. You know he brought us up right. Mum wouldn't never have had a letter if he hadn't showed us how."

Andy knew this was true but he still hated writing letters.

"All right, don't carry on. I'll write but it will be short Anyway Mum can't read a long letter."

At Rose Cottage it was clear something odd was going on. Outside the door there was a van out of which a man was helping an older edition of Mrs. Seecom. Mrs. Seecom was on the doorstep supervising.

"Hullo, kiddies!" she said in an unusually welcoming voice. "This is my mum, Dulcie's grandma, and in the back when we open it up is my dad. This"—with a gesture she pointed out the man helping Dulcie's grandmother out of the van—"is Mr. Seecom, Dulcie's daddy."

The grandmother paused and looked at the children. Then she turned to her daughter.

"The van will be O.K. for them. Be fun sleepin' out for a night or two, won't it, kiddies?"

Mrs. Seecom looked as if she wished her mother would keep quiet.

"That's enough, Mum. Nothing's fixed yet."

Dulcie's father had a curious rough voice as though all his life he had been shouting.

"Clara's right, Mum. You wait till I get going on those locked doors. I've never known one yet I couldn't beat."

The old lady safely in the house, Dulcie's father opened the back of the van and pulled out a thin little man who seemed to have been asleep and did not want to wake up.

"Was it?" he asked crossly.

"We're here," Dulcie's father explained. "Come on, you boys, give him an arm. He's full of beer. We don't want 'im fallin' over."

Laura watched Andy and Tim steer Dulcie's grandfather into the house. Living in Mansfield Road she had often seen men and women who had drunk too much. But that was long ago. In the world of Sir and the Elks it didn't happen. She was sure none of what was going on should be happening now. What was this talk of them sleeping in the van? Was there anything she ought to do?

"Come on, girlie," said Dulcie's father. "Don't stand there dreamin'. Take this box in. There's a smashin' basin of jellied eels in it. They'll make your hair curl."

The Key

M R S. S E E C O M was nobody's fool. This was her big moment to make up to her family for her previous failures to get them put up for weekends. All her family was the same; and it was always more fun to be a crowd than a few. There were no end of laughs to be had if you squeezed in more people than a house could hold. So Mrs. Seecom, waiting until Laura was out of the way, tackled the boys. They were at that moment watching spellbound as Dulcie's father, whose name was Syd, with various tools and bits of wire, tried to open the lounge door.

"How's it going?" she asked.

Syd cleared his husky voice.

"Not too good I'm afraid. This is one of those fancy locks. And I don't like to damage it permanent."

Tim was skipping with excitement.

"Syd says if he can open it he'll learn us how to do it."

"That'll be nice," said Mrs. Seecom. "You never know when it will come in useful. What I came to ask was how you boys and Laura, of course, would fancy sleeping in the back of the van."

Syd's voice broke in.

"Very comfortable that can be. We put in a couple of mattresses and a lot of blankets in case."

The boys did not need to hear about mattresses and blankets. It was enough to know they were to sleep in a van.

"How smashin'!" said Andy. "Can I tell Laura?"

"Where's Dulcie goin'?" Syd asked.

Mrs. Seecom sounded as if she was handing out presents.

"In the van too unless you can open that door."

Syd got up off the floor and put his tools and wire away in his pocket.

"I'm wastin' me time. I'm glad her that owns this house isn't here. Such meanness locking doors in wartime. She should be glad to give those who suffer the bombing each night a bit of shut-eye."

"What about the windows?" Mrs. Seecom asked.

Syd shook his head.

"Done up so tight they wouldn't open if a bomb burst near them."

The boys thought the arrival of the Seecom relations was a great success. Out of bags and suitcases they produced all kinds of food bought on the black market. The jellied eels were delicious, and to finish off the meal there was a glory the children had never seen—a huge box of chocolates tied with ribbon. For the grownups there were all types of drink and for the children blackcurrant juice, the sort kept for babies.

After supper, led by Dulcie, there was dancing in the passage and on the stairs. Laura did not join in the dancing. On Mrs. Seecom's instructions she was doing the washing up with Dulcie's grandma. This time she washed and

Grandma dried. For quite a while they said nothing for there was enough noise outside.

Then Dulcie's grandma said, "You're a funny silent little piece. What are you thinking?"

Laura was so confused she did not know what she was thinking. All the months they had lived with Sir and the Elks had taught her a great deal without her knowing it. Not just using a toothbrush and things like that, but to be polite, to speak quietly, and quite a lot about right and wrong. Not that she had not learned about right and wrong at home—she had. Nobby was very particular about honesty and so was Rosie in a different way. What would they say about what was going on now? Trying to open locked doors. Telling everybody how clever they were at getting more than their rations. Sir would have been very down on that. Yet nobody was doing any real harm and, knowing now about air raids, she could see it was nice to get a quiet night if you could. She told Dulcie's grandma a part of the truth.

"I was thinking about Miss Justworthy, whose house this is. I wonder what she'd say if she could see Rose Cottage now."

Dulcie's grandma gave a deep chuckle that rumbled all through her.

"What the eye can't see the 'eart can't grieve after. That's always been my motto. There she's lyin' comfortable in bed with nurses lookin' after 'er so thank Gawd she doesn't know nor ever will. Mrs. Seecom as you call 'er—but she's Clara to me—is a rare hand at tidying up. After we've gone you'd never know we'd put a foot in the place."

Laura was glad to hear that, but she was still kind of fussed inside. If only she had not got to go and see Miss Justworthy on Sunday. What was she to say if Miss Justworthy asked questions? How awful if anybody noticed the extra people in the house and told Miss Justworthy. She was sure she would be blamed. She would be told she should have reported what was going on to somebody, that's what Mrs. Elk would say. But report to who? You couldn't tell the police about people who had given you all those beautiful chocolates.

Sleeping in the van was rather fun and quite comfortable. Dulcie and Laura shared one mattress, and the boys the other. Dulcie in bed was quite different from the bouncing Dulcie of the daytime. She told Laura all about her stage school and what fun it was and how much she missed it.

"Mum makes me practice every day but it's not like going to school. I could be making mistakes which could ruin my feet."

"Can't they learn you at the school and that?" Laura asked.

"No. They don't know nothin' about it. But Mum's promised the minute the bombin' stops we can go 'ome. Our house is gone but we'll fit in with one of the family."

Dulcie said a lot more, but Laura went to sleep in the middle of it. She must have heard some of what Dulcie said, for she dreamed she was turning cartwheel after cartwheel, which was very nice, for awake she couldn't turn one.

The Seecom relations were still there on Sunday. It seemed they were planning to leave on Monday. Food and drink still flowed and so did petrol, so Syd was always taking some of them out for drives. The boys adored Syd, and Andy openly lamented he had not been able to open the locked doors and blamed the meanness of Miss Justworthy. Laura was shocked but she could see it was no good saying so while the visitors were there. She would leave it until they were on their own again with only Mrs. Seecom and Dulcie for company.

On Sunday Syd produced an unexpected treat. A joint of beef. What the Seecoms liked was a big sit-down Sunday lunch about half past two. This was of course no good to Laura, who had to be at the cottage hospital at three. Somehow Laura, who was no good at deceiving anybody, had managed to keep from almost everybody that she was going to the hospital. She would have told the boys, but in their present mood they would be bound to tell Syd. In the end she had confided in Dulcie.

Dulcie had giggled when she heard.

"Don't let my mum know or she won't half create. She'll be scared you'll tell Miss Justworthy that Dad and Grandma and Grandpa are staying."

"But what shall I tell 'er? Your mum's sure to notice I'm not here."

Dulcie had put her mind to the problem.

"What d'you generally do of a Sunday?"

"Before Sir was dead we went to church along of him. Then after he died we was usually taken by Mrs. Elk to the children's service. Sunday afternoon that is."

"Well, that's it. That's where you've gone. I'll see your dinner's kept 'ot in the oven."

Laura could not feel Sir would entirely have approved this deception, but Mum wouldn't mind. She'd see at once that it was no good upsetting Mrs. Seecom.

As it happened Dulcie managed the affair superbly.

"Put a plate for Laura in the oven, Gran," she shouted above the noise round the table.

"Where's she then?" Dulcie's grandma asked.

They were all talking at once, telling jokes and helping

each other to Yorkshire pudding made with real eggs.

"Catch me eating that powdered stuff," said Dulcie's grandfather. That made all his family laugh.

"By the time you come to the table you've got so much liquid refreshment in you you wouldn't know if you was eatin' ostrich eggs."

"Where's Laura then?" Grandma repeated.

Dulcie managed to sound smug.

"Where d'you think on a Sunday? Church, a'course."

The subject of Laura dropped like a stone. She was in church; she would eat her dinner later. What was wrong with that?

Miss Justworthy was sitting up in bed wearing a bright-blue bed jacket she had knitted herself. Somehow brisk Miss Justworthy looked all wrong in a bed. She should be giving orders and riding on her bicycle. However, as soon as she spoke her authoritative voice was back.

"Sit down, Laura. I hope you and the boys are comfortable. Is Mrs. Seecom keeping my house nicely?"

Laura could say with truth that usually Mrs. Seecom did. Of course this weekend it was a mess with Dulcie's grandpa and grandma smoking without stopping in the spare room. Even Mrs. Seecom had said, "What a smell! It'll take me a week to air the place."

Then, of course, with so many for meals there was no time to clear the kitchen properly. Still, it would be cleaned when the family had gone.

"Yes. She's very fond of cleaning."

"Good. I hope you three help. In wartime everybody must do what they can."

"That's what Sir always said, but it's not so easy at Rose Cottage. Now we sit in the kitchen. There's no fire so Andy can't cut logs, and no garden for Tim to help with the diggin' and . . ."

Miss Justworthy felt this was intended to show Rose Cottage was inferior to Small Hall. Abruptly she changed the subject.

"Now, Laura, attend to me. I do not like trusting my keys to anyone, but Mrs. Elk always spoke highly of you so I am going to trust you." She held out a key. "This is the key of my lounge. Wait until everybody is out then unlock the door. Straight in front of you there is a glass cabinet full of small china objects bearing the crests of various towns. I have made a collection of such things. The cabinet is not locked. It has one drawer. Open that and on the top you will see a piece of paper on which is the Elks' address. Make a copy of it then close the drawer and relock the room. Then, as soon as possible in this envelope," Miss Justworthy held up an envelope addressed to herself, "return the key to me."

Laura repeated the instructions, then carefully put the envelope with the key in it in her pocket.

Miss Justworthy became her usual self.

"You have already been severely scolded for the trouble you caused in running away, and I understand from your teacher you are very ashamed. So I will say no more about that disgraceful episode. I understand you saw your mother. Did she or the hospital give you any idea when she may be allowed out?"

"There was a W.V.S. lady, a Mrs. Hallow, and she told us Mum would need convalescence. She said when that was over they would 'ave to start lookin' for a new 'ouse for us. So when Dad comes 'ome we could all be together again like. But it can't be London. Mum won't let us stay there and she says Dad wouldn't neither."

Miss Justworthy smothered a sigh. It looked as though the Clark children would be on her hands for a long time yet.

"Well, that's all, Laura. You can go. I believe I ought to be home in perhaps two weeks. Now don't forget to return that key."

After so big a lunch all the growups seemed to have gone to sleep when Laura got home. Dulcie, however, was about. She shoved her arm through Laura's the moment she opened the gate of Rose Cottage.

"Go off all right?"

Laura showed her the envelope.

"The key is in this, I got to return it."

Dulcie giggled.

"What my mum would give to lay her hands on that! Come on, your dinner's in the oven."

"Where's the boys?" asked Laura.

"Being sick somewhere I wouldn't wonder. Dad gave them a great load of sweets to keep 'em quiet."

Laura started to move.

"I better go and find them. Andy isn't never sick but Tim throws up ever so easily."

Dulcie gripped her arm.

"Leave 'em alone. Throwin' up never hurt nobody. Besides, now might be just the right moment to get that address. Wait till I see if Mum's asleep."

Dulcie left Laura to get her food out of the oven while she crept upstairs. Her father was snoring and her mother making little bubbling sounds. It was clear both were asleep. Dulcie ran quietly back to the kitchen.

"Go on. I'll keep watch. If I call out, lock the door again and hide the key. Even swallow it if you must."

It was all as Miss Justworthy had said it would be. There

was the cabinet full of little mugs, ashtrays, and small boxes each bearing a colored crest round which was painted "A present from Ilfracombe, Brighton" or whatever town Miss Justworthy had visited. Underneath was the unlocked drawer, and on a piece of paper neatly printed by Elk their address. Laura had armed herself with a piece of paper and a pencil, so she carefully copied the address, then put the original back in the drawer. She was just going to put her copy in her pocket when in a very loud voice Dulcie said, "Hullo, Mum. I thought you were asleep."

Quiet as a mouse Laura moved to the door. It was ajar with the key outside.

Dulcie said loudly, "Come on, Mum. You still look half asleep. I'll make you a cuppa."

Laura, her ear to the door, heard footsteps. It sounded as though Mrs. Seecom was moving into the kitchen. Then she heard the kitchen door shut. In one second she was out of the lounge, had locked the door, and had hidden the key in its envelope under her mattress in the van. Then, trying to look like someone coming straight from church, she hurried to the kitchen.

News of Dad

LAURA, having wolfed her lunch for she was ravenous, managed to escape from the kitchen before Mrs. Seecom gave her a list of things to do. The boys were out playing on the green so Laura had the van to herself. She took the pad of writing paper and the stamps from where she and the boys had put them and settled down to try and write a really good letter to the Elks.

> Dere Mister and Mises Elk we are all well its not nice here without you but there is a Mises Seecom looks after us in Miss Justworthy's house and she is not too bad but we think Miss Justworthy would have a fit if she saw her house now she has locked up the lounge and the dining room so outside the kitchen there is only the two bedrooms. In the one meant for us Mises Seecom's old mum sleeps and her husband he drinks beer all day. Mrs. Seecom and her husband Sid sleep in the other. We like him. They go tomorrer will write again soon. Love Laura.

She stamped the letter and ran to the post box and posted it.

In the village what was to become known as the "goin's on" at Rose Cottage had not passed unnoticed. So on the Monday afternoon not long after the van had left, and while Mrs. Seecom was getting the house into its usual state of tidiness, Mr. Silt, the warden, came up the garden path. In answer to his knock Mrs. Seecom came to the door. She gave Mr. Silt what she hoped was a welcoming smile. It was not—it was more like the smile the wolf gave to Red Riding Hood—but Mr. Silt did not notice. Dealing with evacuees was not his job, and he thought of nothing but getting this visit over as soon as possible.

"It has been brought to our notice that last Saturday and Sunday there was visitors in this house. By the arrangement made with the county billeting officer all that could stay here was you and your child."

Mrs. Seecom thought quickly. Who had reported her? She dismissed the idea it might have been the children. The boys had enjoyed themselves and hoped for more visitors next weekend, and that quiet little Laura wouldn't say anything. No, it must be the neighbors. Spiteful cats!

Her voice sounded as though it was soaked in cream.

"That's easily explained. My old mother has been badly shaken by the bombing. Well, you know how bad it's been lately so, though she only came down for the day to see me and my little girl, she just collapsed and wasn't fit to go back. So I made her stay. I gave her and my dad my room, and Dulcie and I and my husband slept in my husband's van. Well, what would you have done, warden? Would you have turned out a bomb-shocked old woman?"

The warden felt he was not being told the truth but, as

far as he could see, no harm had been done. He was taken in and shown the two bedrooms and the kitchen and bathroom, all of which seemed to him to be in order, though Mrs. Seecom said the stove needed a good clean. So he said grudgingly:

"Seems O.K. to me but there must be no more complaints. This is a borrowed house, remember."

So, much to the boys' disappointment, that next weekend none of the family came down. Dulcie told Laura what had happened.

"Mum daren't let them come, not with that warden watchin' the house."

As it happened, by the third Sunday Miss Justworthy was home—very shaky and not able to do much, but definitely mistress of her own house. It was clear to everybody she would not get on with Mrs. Seecom, and there had been a lot of telephoning trying to find beds for her and Dulcie. Then, to everyone's surprise and relief, Mrs. Seecom made her own plans.

"We're going back to London on Sunday," she told Miss Justworthy's replacement as billeting officer. "They've had no bombs for nearly a week now and they say *that Hitler* has given up trying to smash London."

Mrs. Seecom did everything very correctly. She stayed to look after the children until a Civil Defense car delivered Miss Justworthy to the door. Then she and Dulcie got into the local taxi and drove to the station.

"We'll meet again," Dulcie said, saying good-by to the Clarks. "All you got to do is to watch the posters. Won't be long now before my name is up in lights."

During the following months Laura and Miss Justworthy sort of became friends. Miss Justworthy remained somewhat frail as the result of her accident and really grateful for Laura's efforts to help. Mrs. Elk had taught Laura only rudimentary cooking but she had taught her well, so Laura took over the main meal, which was after school and was called supper. She also helped with the housework and even persuaded Andy and Tim to try to be tidy. No one could say Rose Cottage was a happy home but at least it kept going without any real rows. The children did the shopping, so the question of cat's meat never came up.

Most Sundays the children wrote to Rosie. She was now quite recovered but still in the same hospital working as a ward maid. Andy and Tim wrote their mother only a few lines. Laura told her what news there was to tell. Beaty in reply wrote every week from Rosie, and from these letters the children knew they were still a long way from going home. Rooms or cottages outside London seemed impossible to find.

> *I get postcards, the government sort, which tell you nothing, fairly regularly from your dad. He says he'll be home later this year. The bombs have stopped and we could get a house in London but everyone says don't—there is worse to come. I know you don't like it all that much in Rose Cottage but it won't be long now . . .*

The year 1942 was forever afterwards known by all the children in Charnbury as American year. In December 1941 the Japanese had bombed a place called Pearl Harbor. Colonel Stranger Stranger being dead the children had not heard of this at the time, but it had the effect, so they learned, of bringing the Americans into the war. This, they were told, was because the Japanese were allies of the Germans, so the Americans too were enemies of the Germans. Apparently, according to the school, this meant that thousands of Americans were coming to England to help finish the war. So every patriotic Briton should be ready to welcome them. As a start all in the school must learn to sing "The Star-Spangled Banner."

Unfortunately no one in the school had heard the American anthem played and, in any case, of all anthems it is one of the most difficult to sing. But master it the children had to before the first Americans arrived.

The first Americans arrived in the summer. Because they wore big white tin hats, the nation christened them Snowdrops. They were in fact military police.

When the first few arrived they were a puzzle to Charnbury. The Americans seemed embarrassed at the children's attempt to sing "The Star-Spangled Banner." They did not like being called Sir. They did not want parties given for them. What they liked was being called names like Bud, being treated as one of the family, and being allowed to drop into friends' houses without formality. And if there was a job of work wanted doing, so much the better.

There were also things the Americans refused to do. Nothing would make them share the villagers' meager food rations. Instead they gave, and how they gave! In no time they had taught the children to chew gum and handed pieces out to any child who asked for it. They also gave the children chocolates so, without meaning any harm, they taught the children to beg. "Got any gum, chum?" became part of every child's vocabulary.

In the homes, they arrived with luxuries the villagers had not seen for years. But it was not the presents the villagers came to love; it was the Americans.

The Americans, after the first few had settled down, came in hundreds, and soon the village knew why. It was, of course, a secret and must not be talked about, but they were building an airfield. Just one thing could be mentioned: one of the big buildings they were putting up was what the Americans called a movie house. It seemed someone called Uncle Sam gave all the troops movie houses, but they would be shared. Perhaps two nights a week everybody would be invited to see the pictures. Charnbury could not believe in its good fortune. "We shan't half miss them when they go away," the villagers said and it proved quite true.

All that year, in spite of the Americans arriving, the news was bad. With no Colonel Stranger Stranger to tell them what was going on the children only picked up news in scraps, but they could of course feel the grownups were worried. Laura knew, because the Americans said so, the Japanese in the Far East had taken most of the places colored pink on the map, and had sunk a lot of ships doing it. Beaty must have guessed the children would hear about what the Japanese were doing, for in one of the letters she wrote for Rosie she added a P.S.: "I don't think you need worry about your dad, for, from what your mum says, he's nowhere near the Japs."

Christmas that year was wonderful. The plan was that the British should entertain the Americans. For this an entertainment was to be put on in the Scouts' Hut. The high spot of this was to be a nativity play, followed by a party for which every woman in the village made cakes and a lady in the W.V.S. was borrowed because she could make coffee as it was made in America. What the villagers called "our Americans" had given up drinking coffee as made in Charnbury. Instead, they had taken to drinking tea.

For Laura this party for the Americans was the most exciting thing she could remember, for she was chosen to be Mary in the nativity play. Nobody argued about Laura's being chosen, for all the village agreed she "looked the part."

Miss Justworthy was the only one who did not like Laura's being selected.

"If they think I'm going to make your dress they're all wrong. I've got too much to do as it is. So don't bring any patterns back here."

Laura was scared that not being able to get her dress made at home might lose her the part, but it was all right. All clothes were rationed so there was no one in the village who could spare anything. "Us is already a mass of patches," they explained. All the same a lot can be done with imagination. Laura, dressed in the white skirt someone had worn as part of a fancy dress, a white jersey with a high neck, her face bound in white handkerchiefs so no hair was visible, and with a blue quilt, sent from Canada for the homeless, draped over her head and touching the floor, looked, as many said, "just like she came off a Christmas card." Andy was tried out as one of the shepherds, but he wouldn't remember his lines so he lost the part. Tim was a boy angel. He hated it but he had no choice. He loathed wearing wings and a halo.

The Americans were wonderful guests, managing to seem pleased with everything. At the end of the party an officer got up and thanked everybody. Then he asked the whole village to a party at the camp on New Year's Day.

What a party that was! There was a Christmas tree up to the roof with wonderful presents for everybody on it. There was an enormous tea with masses of iced cakes. There was a

Walt Disney film, and before they left the Americans gave every child a box of what they had called sweets but were learning to call candy.

It was a good thing Christmas was so nice because right afterwards there was bad news. It was told to the children by Miss Justworthy. She probably tried hard to tell them gently, but even when she tried to be gentle she sounded as though she was giving orders. It was after breakfast when the post came. The children were supposed to be helping in the house before they went out to do the shopping, for their school was back in the afternoons. Miss Justworthy called them into the lounge. She had a letter in her hand.

"I have heard from your mother—or rather the friend who writes for her. She has heard from the Admiralty. Your father is in hospital. He is suffering from frostbite."

"What's that?" Andy asked.

Miss Justworthy was vague.

"I've read about cases, of course, but never actually seen one. I believe it comes from the cold. It stops the blood flowing in the affected part."

Laura said, "Where is Dad?"

"They've landed him at a hospital in the north of Scotland. Your mother has gone to see him. She says she would have liked to take you children but she doubts if they'd let her."

There were two weeks after that without any letters. Then one came from Beaty for Miss Justworthy. The children did not see this, but Miss Justworthy told them some of what it said.

"Your mother says your father has been very ill. He's been on the danger list." Then came the terrible bit. "He's better now, but they have had to cut off his right leg."

The End

THE ELKS heard this news about the children's father from Laura. She had only been able to give Mrs. Elk the bare facts. She had no ability to tell her of the effect of the news on all of them. How Andy several nights running had waked up screaming. How Tim was always near tears, saying, "I wish we could see Mum." Still less of the cold feeling inside which never left her since the news had come. For all three knew at first hand what it was like to lose a leg. A man who had lived in Mansfield Road had lost a leg in what was called the First World War. He was, so his wife told anybody who would listen, in terrible pain day and night and would never be able to work again.

This sad man had stayed in all the children's minds. He was somehow frightening. His memory scared Laura and Andy, who had once found him leaning against a wall crying. They had never before seen a grown-up man cry. "Run along, kids," he had sobbed. "Don't mind me. If I knew a way I'd kill myself. Straight I would."

Laura was sure, without asking him, that Andy was as

scared as she was that Dad was feeling like that. But he musn't kill himself. They must get to him first. But how! Who was there who would help?

Laura thought and thought what to do until she felt like a moth caught in a light, battering to find a way out. Miss Justworthy wasn't the sort anybody could talk to. There were the teachers at school. They were kind, but with two schools going, one in the morning and one in the afternoon, they had no time to talk to anybody. If only the Elks were get-at-able, but they were not. They lived miles away, and though they did not grumble in their letters, it was clear they felt unhappy squashed into Mr. Elk's mother's cottage.

Then one day in school when Laura should have been giving her mind to geography she remembered someone. Someone who was used to helping and always knew how to do it: Mrs. Hallow. After school, not waiting for second thoughts, she got out their notepaper and wrote to Mrs. Hallow. Having no address she put W.V.S. after Mrs. Hallow's name and sent the letter to the Town Hall.

> *Dere Mises Hallow our Dad has had his leg cut off he is in hospital in Skotland. Mum is there too. We want to see our Dad bad for he must not kill himself. Laura Clark.*

In time the letter reached Mrs. Hallow. In spite of all the people she had looked after since she befriended the Clark children, she remembered them. "Laura, Andy, and Tim," she murmured. Then she reread the letter and puzzled how best she could help. One of the great difficulties in wartime was one that affected everybody. All the things which had to do with civilians and even the pets of civilians, such as dogs,

belonged to different departments. All the departments
worked on the whole very well together, unless one depart-
ment interfered in something which should have belonged to
another. Then there was all too often a row. "Now," wondered Mrs. Hallow, "to whom does arranging to get the
Clark children to see their father belong? Refugees? The
Red Cross? Civil Defense? The police?" She must take
advice.

Mrs. Hallow went to see her old friend Colonel Ponsonby,
but he stopped her before she had time to read to him Laura's
letter.

"One minute, me dear." He started to rummage among
the papers on his desk. "Elk," he said, "old Launcelot
Stranger Stranger's valet."

Mrs. Hallow looked at him admiringly.

"Did you get in touch with him? You said you thought it
was a line worth following."

Colonel Ponsonby found the paper he was looking for.

"Tell you the truth it wasn't me that did something about
it. It was Elk. There was a photograph of me at a Civil
Defense affair. Seems Elk saw it and had the sense to write
to me. Listen."

> *Dear Sir,*
>   *I saw your photo in the paper at a Civil Defense
> affair. You will not remember me but you will I
> know remember Colonel Stranger Stranger who I
> regret to say died some time ago. We buried him
> with military honors. The Colonel left me a nice
> little cottage but I could not live in it at the time
> as there was land girls in it. Now I hear the Amer-
> icans need Gedge's farm for military purposes so*

my cottage is empty. That is why I am presuming to write to you. Could you tell me if we took in the Clark children as evacuees could I claim my cottage?

"That will be wonderful," said Mrs. Hallow, "but now read Laura's letter. Through whom do I arrange to get the children to Scotland?"

Colonel Ponsonby read the letter. Then he laid it down amongst his papers.

"The Lord moves in a mysterious way. At this moment the Admiralty are interesting themselves in the case of Able Seaman Clark. It seems on a Russian convoy he dived to the rescue of his officer. That was how he got the frostbite which cost him his leg. The Admiralty hope he will be decorated."

"How splendid! But what about the children? Can I get them to Scotland?"

"We have a better plan than that. We are trying to arrange that Able Seaman Clark, and his wife, plus of course the children, all share the cottage with the Elks."

Anything to do with government departments takes a very long time to arrange. But one day that summer it all happened. First, the land girls moved out of the cottage to Mr. Gedge's new farm. Then the Elks arrived. The land girls had done their best to leave the place tidy but to Mrs. Elk it was a poor best. She took two weeks to get the cottage to her idea of perfect condition. Then one day Miss Justworthy drove the children over. Good-bys to her were very brief, for neither the children nor Miss Justworthy could pretend they were sorry to say good-by.

It was a day later that the ambulance arrived. The children had all braced themselves for the change there would be in their father. Laura had even imagined him arriving crying. But they were in for a shock. Without help from anybody, Nobby, grinning from ear to ear, hopped out of the ambulance. He had of course one false leg but it didn't show, and though he had a stick it was clear he despised it.

"Hullo, kids," he said. "This is a bit of all right." Then he saw the cottage. "It's a lot better than what Hitler blew away."

Rosie said to Elk, "He reckons he'll learn to be a farmer."

Martha beamed.

"I wish the Colonel was here to see us now. He wouldn't half be pleased. I know the war's not over and there may be worse to come, but we've managed so far so I reckon we'll manage to the end."

About the Author:

NOEL STREATFEILD's first book for children, *Ballet Shoes*, appeared in America in 1937 and was an immediate success. Since then she has written more than a dozen popular books for young readers, as well as several distinguished works for adults. Her last juvenile novel for Random House was *Thursday's Child*, called "a fresh and sprightly addition to a perennially popular genre" by *Horn Book* and described as "immensely satisfying and involving" by the ALA *Booklist*.
When the Sirens Wailed is Noel Streatfeild's first World War II story since the ones she wrote during the war itself. In writing this novel she has drawn on the vivid memories of her own experiences in the Women's Voluntary Service. Miss Streatfeild lives in London.

About the Artist:

JUDITH GWYN BROWN is the distinguished illustrator of more than forty books for young readers, including *Mandy* by Julie Edwards. Her drawings are in the collections of the Metropolitan Museum of Art in New York City and in the Huntington Library in California. Miss Brown lives in New York City.